The KITES *of* LOVE

ENADENE MCFARLANE

ISBN 978-1-68517-583-2 (paperback)
ISBN 978-1-68517-584-9 (digital)

Christian Faith Publishing
832 Park Avenue
Meadville, PA 16335
www.christianfaithpublishing.com

Printed in the United States of America

INTRODUCTION

Maud was born in Jamaica, an island in the West Indies. She grew up in the rural parishes of Jamaica. She was an only child—no siblings, only distant relatives. Her parents left her when she was three years old. She had no memory of her mother. The only attachment from mother to daughter was the lingering scent from her mother's bosom that she remembered. Her parents immigrated to Cuba for plantation work after nursing her for three years of her life. Her grandmother later raised Maud. The scent from her mother's bosom lingered on for years then transformed as a desire to find her mother and father.

CHAPTER 1

Maud was born in 1906 in Jamaica as a female child. Her parents, Jonathan and Annamay, were happy to bring her into the world.

Jon and Ann, as they would refer to each other, were common-law husband and wife. They were not legally bound but assumed this status.

Jon was in his early thirties—thirty-two years old—a stature of 6'2", with light brown complexion. He was a mulatto and had a body mass of 190 lbs. His family came from Africa, five generations of slavery. His parents were free but were still in bondage, subject to their master's rigid rules and regulation while working on the plantation. His parents, tired of the mistreatment by their master, pooled the meager wages and bought a piece of uncultivated land in the parish of Saint Mary. The one-acre piece of land they purchased had many trees, clusters of lignum vitae, bamboo, and fruit trees.

Jon inherited the land and house when his parents died. He was an only child; his other siblings died during childbirth. Jon moved Ann in four months after their courtship.

Jon was functionally illiterate and lacked skills. He had limited knowledge of cultivating, which he learned from working side by side in the field with his parents.

With limited skills, Jon had difficulty finding work to support his family. He went out early in the morning till dusk to look for work but was unsuccessful in finding a job. As his daughter got older and weaned off from breastfeeding, it became harder to feed three people. The garden was almost empty, and so were the little savings he hid under the mattress. Jon cried to his wife and expressed his frustrations. His wife told him that she heard some gossip going around town: they were hiring for plantation workers in Cuba.

"Oh well," Jon uttered dismally. "I'm not crossing the sea to go to Cuba, leaving you and the baby alone. I would rather go to other parishes to find work."

* * *

Jamaica is an island surrounded by the Caribbean Sea, mapped into fourteen parishes, with a population of approximately six hundred thousand in the early twentieth century.

Jon had to find some way to put food on the table before he went searching for work in the other parishes. Jon had a hard decision to make when he cut down two of the lignum vitae trees in his yard. His tears and sweat ran down the trunks of each tree as he cut them down. Wood of life, the lignum tree is one of the hardest woods and most valuable in Jamaica. They used the flower of the lignum vitae tree for many health issues.

Jon sold the tree trunks as lumber. He needed the money to travel to the other thirteen parishes to find work. Jon gave Ann a portion of the sale from the lumber to take care of her and the baby. He took the balance with him and set out in his pursuit.

Ann agreed with her husband to go out of parish to find work. She could manage on her own for a while.

Ann's foreparents of African descent came from Africa as slaves to Jamaica. Ann was very tall for a woman, standing at seventy inches, four inches shorter than her husband. Her rich dark-brown complexion made her insanely beautiful. Ann was literate, completing school at fifteen years old. After finishing school, Ann's mother contracted with the neighbor living in the district, bartering for dressmaking lessons for Ann to help in her field. Ann became a skilled seamstress by trade. Ann's father left her mother when she was a child, raised solely by her mother. It was a woman's place to take care of the house and raise the children. Ann had no memory of her father. The disappearance of her father, leaving the matrimonial home, devastated her mother and scarred her for life. Her mother never took on another companion or had other children. Ann was an only child. Her mother gave her undivided love and attention and encouraged her to read the Bible when she wasn't sewing or working in the field.

Ann's mother taught her everything, from a woman's place in the home, cooking and taking care of the house, to a man's job, working in the field. She passed on her knowledge, molding her for the outside world.

Ann developed toned muscles for long hours working in the field and wasn't afraid of a challenge. She took care of the house and the yard, keeping up with the repairs and cleaning. Ann budgeted the money Jon gave her, pinching needs over her wants, only buying food for her and Maud.

* * *

It had been six months since Jon left. Ann was getting worried. She missed her husband but had a part of him—their daughter, Maud. Jon was missing out on Maud's walking and babbling pieces of words. The two spent a lot of time together, Maud falling asleep in her bosom.

It was hard to write letters when he was traveling from one parish to the next. Ann comforted herself with positive thoughts, reading the Bible and keeping her faith strong. There was nothing she could do but wait.

Jon came home three months later, after nine months of being away from his family. Ann could barely recognize her husband. He was twenty-five pounds thinner and three shades darker. Jon relayed his misadventure. He got some work for a day, sometimes a few hours, nothing substantial. He slept with friends, sometimes on the side of the road.

"It was tough!" he remarked. Jon came back with lesser money than he went. He was angry at himself for leaving his family for so long and came back less of a man. But he had to try.

Weeks turned into months. Life wasn't getting any better. Something had to give. Jon considered Ann's gossip and sought if it was true or just a gossip. He got up early one morning and walked to Saint Ann's Bay in the parish of Saint Ann.

Saint Ann borders Saint Mary, which was a more striving parish than Saint Mary.

Jon went to the police station and spoke with the constable. He received the information as to be true. They were hiring immigrants to migrate to Cuba for plantation work. The constable gave Jon the information he needed. Jon had a lot of time to think on the seven-mile walk home. Seven hundred thoughts running through his mind, his thoughts poured out in sweat on his head, running down his face. He shaded under a tree and held his hand to his head as if trying to sort out his thoughts in chronological order. He rambled out aloud, "Oh, my family, it will be hard to leave you."

Jon arrived home later that evening. The walk from town to his home was a fifteen-mile round trip. Jon washed up and had dinner. He then had a hard talk with his wife. The conversation led to him making a better living for him and his family and considering going to Cuba, if that's what it takes. Ann could hear the crack in his voice of anxiety; he was nervous.

She pulled her chair closer then looked up at him with tearful eyes; she felt his pain. The stress and sleepless nights caused his eyes to sink in the back of his head. It broke him down, trying to make a life for his family. She covered her husband's hand with hers, consoling him. "It will be fine. You could go to Cuba," she said as tears flowed down her dirt-filled face like muddy water.

Ann worked in the garden earlier that day and was filled with earth from her hair to her bare feet. She was dirty and smelled like rotten mulch. Ann took a bath five days ago and wasn't ready for another bath for another two days. She only took a bath once a week, and so did Jon. He also hadn't taken a bath for almost two weeks. It was the norm; they thought nothing of it. They had each other.

Jon told Ann that he would sign up.

Ann looked on. She thought to herself, *I would like to go.* The thoughts trickled down from her brain into her mouth. The words flowing through her lips filled the room like steam being released from a boiling pot. She was ready to go. Jon opened his mouth to speak. His jaw locked in place in astonishment. He was speechless. The poverty-stricken life was getting to her too. Ann wanted to make a difference. Her dressmaking skill wasn't bringing in any work.

Ann was an ambitious youthful woman. Laziness was never in her vocabulary. She would work alongside her husband, or any man, toe-to-toe. Ann reminded her husband of her industrious nature, trying to convince him to let her go with him to Cuba. She went on a long stretch like a politician trying to make her case. "I have helped build the addition to the house we live in accommodating Maud's birth," she said. The lumber used for making the addition were trees from their yard. "I helped cut trees down, sawed to cut the lumber for beams and sidings, and watered down the earth to make the floor hard like concrete," she continued.

"I made the mattress from dried coconut husks, embodied in a cloth sack, and the pillows from dried coconut husks too." Ann knew her skills and ambition would be an asset. Ann begged Jon to let her go. After much debate, he gave in, agreeing that she could go with him. Ann was ecstatic, smiling from ear to ear.

Ann planned with her mother to keep Maud, stating that she would only go to Cuba for a year, and Jon would stay a year or two longer, depending on the demand.

* * *

Donnann James, sixty-seven years old, Ann's mother, lived next door to her on a half acre of land. She was an independent woman who lived alone for the past thirty years since her common-law husband walked out of their life. Ann's mother goes by the name MamaJames.

MamaJames had fallen into the well one night when she went to fetch some water. She fell into the rope-drawn bucket, headfirst. MamaJames held onto the rope attached to the bucket and pulled herself upright; she stuck both of her legs out with her back against the wall of the well, using her feet as an anchor to prevent herself from falling farther into the well. The narrow walls held her in place for three hours until her daughter rescued her.

Ann would visit, checking on her mother in the morning and evening before she went to bed.

As Ann approached her mother's house, she heard screaming for help. The scream came from the direction of the well. As she approached closer, she recognized the voice of her mother. Ann ran back to her house and got her husband to help. Together they pulled MamaJames out of the well to safety.

MamaJames suffered water damage to her ears, causing her to go deaf in one ear, and it affected her balance and coordination. MamaJames walked with a cane ever since, using it as a third leg to give her balance.

MamaJames welcomed her granddaughter to live with her for company but will miss her daughter very much. It was the two of them for many years after her father left. They had a close mother-daughter relationship.

They accepted Jon and Ann for farmwork in Cuba.

They traveled by mule, pulled cart to Saint Ann's Bay, then caught the boat to Cuba. MamaJames said her goodbyes at their house, and so did Maud. The trip to the ship dock was too far to travel for baby Maud.

Maud showed some sadness, crying more than usual, as if she knew she would not see her mom soon.

CHAPTER 2

Maud was now four years old. Her words were plain. She was a runner, running around like a kid goat. Each morning when Maud would wake up, she would cry.

It took many hours for MamaJames to calm her down. After many months, MamaJames realized that Maud was missing her mother terribly. She took Maud over to her parents' house, hoping she would connect to something in the house and not be so sad. Maud jumped in her mother's bed, sniffing the sheets and the pillow like an inferior animal, trying to connect. She grabbed onto the pillow that smelled like her mother and would not let go, as if to say, "Mama, am not letting you go." There was an enormous smile on her face. The scent she missed was back.

She shouted, "Mama, I love you." Maud held onto the pillow like an oversized doll, her favorite toy. The pillow was almost ten pounds from the filling of the coconut husk, packed tightly just the way Ann liked her pillow: hard. The pillow was the size of Maud. She had difficulty carrying it. She held onto it with all her might, dragging it to the ground.

MamaJames picked up the pillow off the ground to aid Maud in carrying it. Maud screamed, her lungs expanded, "It's mine, my pillow, leave it alone." Maud suddenly muscled up the energy to lift the pillow to her body. The pillow slipped, dragged to the ground several times, but Maud would not let go.

MamaJames noticed a more cheerful Maud. She had a big part of her mother, the pillow. The powerful scent of her mother was hidden in the pillow. Maud would laugh each morning as she got out of bed. This improved their day. MamaJames was happy.

MamaJames received the first letter from her daughter and son-in-law three months after they arrived in Cuba.

Her neighbor brought the letter along with some groceries. He would do this once a month, when he went to town.

MamaJames was so happy. She opened the letter immediately. She read her name on the envelope but couldn't read the contents of the letter. She was illiterate, so she asked her neighbor's son to read the letter. MamaJames smiled with tears of joy running down the sides of her cheek as he read, "We had settled in Pinar del Río and started working the following day." MamaJames pretended to read the letter to

Maud, memorizing the contents, and gave Maud a big kiss as they requested.

* * *

Two years had passed, and Ann hadn't returned. The letters continued to arrive once every three to four months. It stated they were doing fine, but they mentioned nothing of coming home. MamaJames replied to every letter, using her neighbor's son to help her as she dictated what she wanted to say. "We are doing well. Maud was fine and growing like wild weeds."

But this time, the reply letter was different. MamaJames demanded to know when they were coming home.

MamaJames received a reply to her demands. As she waited for the mail, it felt like she was waiting forever; it was five months later. The letter read that they had struck gold, were doing great, leased a piece of land, and built a house. The letter shocked MamaJames. It made her sad; she knew she couldn't relate the contents of the letter to Maud. She knew she should be happy for them but was afraid that she was losing them and may never see her daughter again. She hid the letter from Maud, afraid that when she could read better, she would find out her parents abandoned her.

Maud would talk to her grandmother every chance she got and looked forward to bedtime stories of her mother and father. During the stories, Maud would lie in her bed with her mother's pillow. She circled the sweat stains on the pillow with her fingers. She picked out the dead hairs entwined in the pillow, then stored them in her writing book. It made Maud happy, laughing each time she plucked a hair from the pillow as if connecting to her mama.

Maud had relatives in both parishes, Saint Mary and Saint Ann. She visited during the long summer break from school. Maud played with her cousins occasionally, but her interest was interacting with the grown-ups. Maud was hoping to get all the information of her mother and father. She cherished the stories and was hungry for more. The history she received from her grandmother was good, but her relatives presented a more precise story compared to her grandmother.

As a child, she observed her grandmother's hearing was getting worse. So was her memory, sparingly, with bits and pieces of factual information. She was grateful for the history as she put the pieces of her grandmother's revelation and her relatives together to form an enormous picture in her mind.

Eight years had passed since Ann and Jon left for Cuba. MamaJames hadn't received a letter from her daughter in two years. She was worried that something was seriously wrong and she might never see her daughter and son-in-law again.

* * *

Ann and Jon had lost their jobs at the plantation they arrived at when they left Jamaica. The master sold the plantation and moved back to Spain. The new owners hired younger workers. Jon was allowed to stay on and work. He declined the job without Ann. The master fired Jon and Ann; they had to leave the plantation immediately. After months of no work, they left their home and traveled away to secure a new job on another plantation.

The new plantation came with a two-year contract for all workers to live on the plantation. Conditions at the new plantation were brutal. The workers were treated like slaves, working long hours in severe weather, rain, and heat. Ann couldn't write to her mother; there were no mails in or out. The master restricted writing of letters to keep the workers focused on their job without interference. Ann and Jon realized that they had made a dreadful mistake taking this job. The consequence of not writing letters to her mother worried her. Ann and Jon could only leave the plantation for church. All who attended church was policed by a foreman. The plantation owner secured his workers, reducing the possibility of escaping.

When Ann and Jon's two-year contract was up, the plantation owner refused to honor it. They were paid wages for work done but were denied leaving the plantation. They stayed on the plantation two more months longer than their contracted time. Ann and Jon were fearful that they might never leave. Jon concocted with the foreman after paying him their two months' wages to release them when they went to church. The foreman did, releasing the rein, setting them free. Jon and Ann had a four-hour lead ahead of the master's army of dogs and foremen. The search for Ann and Jon was in high gear. The barking of dogs could be heard miles away.

They stayed away from the road and traveled inland along the riverbanks.

Ann and Jon washed their bodies in the river and stained their clothes with wild bushes growing on the side of the riverbank to ward off the dogs. After two hours, the barking ceased. Ann and Jon felt it was safe and proceeded to their home.

They arrived home two days later to find their home occupied. The lease was up, and the landlord rented the house to cover the lease payment. Jon was so mad to find a stranger living in his house and using their personal stuff. Jon demanded his house back, trying to push his way inside. He shouted, "This is my house. Get out!" The man and his family fought back, letting Jon know that they had legal rights to live there.

Jon and Ann had nowhere to go and slept in the crawl space, the cellar of their house. The following morning, Jon and Ann went to see the landlord. He told them that it would be a week before they could have their house back. He had to get paid for the lease of the land, so he rented the house to satisfy their lease. The tenants shared food with Jon and Ann every morning and evening until the seventh day when they moved out. Jon and Ann got their house back. They were happy that they didn't have to sleep in the cellar anymore.

Jon went back to the plantation, where he and Ann were fired from, and got his job back. Ann spent most of her time at home getting her house organized back to the way she had it. Ann didn't write to her mother as the post office she sent to and received her mails from was close to the plantation they escaped from. She was afraid to travel there and get caught for running away. Jon was home every evening after work. Ann discussed with her husband about moving to another town, where she can write to her mother and maybe find a way to get back to Jamaica. Ann was tired—tired of the conditions, the slavery conditions of the plantation owners—and was more homesick than ever.

CHAPTER 3

Maud was now eleven years old. She was the splitting image of her mother, tall and beautiful. She was an academic scholar. When she wasn't reading, she would help her grandmother around the house and in the garden.

One day, while Maud was cleaning the house, a wooden box sitting in the window fell to the floor. Everything scattered onto the floor: birth certificates, money, other documents, and the letters from her parents.

MamaJames was coming from the outhouse walking toward the house when she heard a scream. She hurried her steps, yelling, "Are you hurt!"

Maud had never seen this box before, and her first instinct was to hide it, putting the box under the bed. "I'm fine, Grandma!" she yelled back.

The box was the size of a wooden baby cradle and weighed about ten pounds. Maud warded off her grandma from coming into the house. "I am cleaning! I will finish soon," she shouted back to her grandma.

MamaJames took a U-turn to the garden. "I'll just finish working in the garden," she replied.

Maud's heart was pounding inside her chest. "Oh my god, that was close." Breathing heavily, she let out a gigantic sigh. "This is a mystery box," she mumbled under her breath. Her thoughts rambled in her head. "Why haven't I seen this box before? Grandma kept it a secret."

Maud pulled the box from under the bed, busted from falling on the clay floor. She was worried that Grandma would be mad at her. Maud tried fixing the box, but it was beyond repair. Maud picked up the wood splinter from the floor. She hurried in case Grandma showed up. Maud hissed in frustration, took her focus from the broken box, and extracted its contents. Like a detective, she combed through the box, looking at everything. There were approximately thirty letters in the box from her mother—her parents. The letters were still in their original envelopes, dated back to when she was three years old. Maud read every letter, some with one page, others with two pages. Maud stormed out of the house as the weight of the letters sat on her shoulders—a weight she couldn't shake off. She was furious.

She walked toward her grandma. Her steps were long and fast. She was angry and felt empty and betrayed. She had a blank stare in her eyes as she stood facing her grandma. She needed answers right now.

MamaJames raised her limp body to an upright stand, with her hands on her hips, as if trying to hold herself in place. "What's the matter, child?" Grandma asked.

Maud cried as her tears streamed down her face. "Why didn't you tell me my mother—parents—weren't coming home? You lied to me. Your answer is always the same: they are doing fine," she screamed at her grandma in anger. She had never done this before. Justifying her actions, she chose not to apologize to her grandma. "Am not a little child, Grandma. I need to know," Maud said. Her voice echoed over the garden into thin air.

MamaJames saw the anger in her granddaughter's face, the action she displayed, and took a more passive path. As she processed her thoughts, she mumbled to herself, "Two wrongs don't make a right."

MamaJames stepped closer to her granddaughter, gave her a hug, and whispered in her ears, "I was just...I was only trying to protect you."

MamaJames dreaded this day coming and hoped it would be later than sooner. She felt Maud's pain and understood. It was the same pain she felt for many years. MamaJames couldn't hold back her emotions. The tears swelled in her eyes as they held onto each other.

"I'm sorry. I tried to make the best for you!" MamaJames said.

Maud was betrayed and hurt and needed to distance herself from the situation. She took a walk. Maud walked toward her parents' house, a half acre from her grandmother's home. As she walked up the road, she could hear laughter and screaming sounds of fun coming from her parents' house. She stopped in front of the house. The laughter was contagious. Maud smiled as she walked into the yard. She saw the neighbor's son, who now resided in her parents' home. He was flying a kite with his younger brother. Maud looked on for a while and noticed they were having fun. She asked if she could join them. "I have never flown a kite before," she said.

Andrew showed Maud how to make a kite using palm leaves' inner stem as the frame, applying fine cord to bind the stems together, then using paper to cover the frame. Maud looked on, observing how patient and attentive he was.

The youthful man was in his mid-twenties and an ambitious man. He leased the house and surrounding property from MamaJames to make a living.

Andrew was a short muscular guy. He worked in the garden and sold his produce on the side of the road and sometimes at the market. Andrew lived alone with his dog; his parents and younger brother lived four acres up the road and would come by occasionally to visit.

Andrew finished making the kite by adding cord and a tail to propel it in the air.

"That's beautiful!" shouted Maud.

The day was good for kite flying with winds thirty miles per hour. Andrew launched the kite. His dog ran with him playfully, as if trying to catch the tail of the kite. The kite took off right away. Maud held on to the cord with Andrew's help, steering the kite over the high trees up into the sky.

All three kites were miles away into the sky. Maud held onto her kite with a big smile on her face. She was having a wonderful time.

Maud remembered Andrew reading the letters from her parents for her grandma. She confronted him. "Why didn't you tell me my parents weren't coming back?"

"Am sorry, Maud. It wasn't my place. Father asked me to read the letters, and that's what I did," said Andrew.

"I understand!" she replied.

Maud forgave Andrew. She had a good time flying kites. She asked Andrew for some palm leaves to take home to make her own kites. Maud thanked Andrew for his help and left for home.

Maud ran down the gravel road, with dust under her heels as her bare feet trampled the earth. Her grandmother waited for her outside the house.

"I was worried sick! Where were you?" MamaJames asked.

MamaJames had time to think when Maud went for her walk. She too needed time to swallow the reality that she hadn't heard from her daughter in a long time. She wasn't coming home.

Time had gone by fast, and so did Maud's growth. She was tall and smart and possessed the ability to read and comprehend. MamaJames did not expect her granddaughter to have this ability at such a young age. She now realized she had to share life experience with her and mend their relationship. After all, they only had each other.

"I was over at Mama's old house, flying kites with the neighbor," Maud replied.

Maud washed up and got ready for dinner. After eating, she told her grandmother of her kite-flying experience. The two had an endless chat. MamaJames's voice was shaky with a tear-filled sound as she spoke of her daughter. It became obvious to Maud that she too was missing her mother. Maud sat by her grandma, trying to comfort her. "It will be all right, Grandma!"

MamaJames was getting old, her body was weak, and she was worried that she wouldn't be able to take care of her granddaughter. MamaJames's mind reflected on Maud's kite-flying adventure with the neighbor. This worried her. She thought, *Maud would be a teenager soon, and with the older male company she was keeping, it could be dangerous.* This thought troubled her. MamaJames had to do whatever it takes to stop Maud visiting the neighbor. Like building blocks, MamaJames's thoughts were piling up. *Maud needed female friends her age to play girls' games.*

MamaJames went to bed after talking to Maud. She was up most of the night, with thoughts running through her mind of their earlier conversations. Her thoughts were like wild tree vines connecting with other thoughts. Her brain was full. She had to empty these thoughts from her brain. It was making her crazy.

MamaJames had a long talk with Maud when she returned from school. They talked of the birds and the bees.

MamaJames decided and voiced her thoughts. "You and I will spend more weekends with our relatives in Saint Ann."

Maud had an enormous smile on her face. She missed her cousins and her other relatives. She asked if it was because of the birds and the bees. "Yes!" MamaJames smiled.

Maud laughed, covering her mouth with her hand as her eyes gleamed with astonishment. Smiling at her own words, MamaJames continued, "You also need other interactions with children your own age, not an old woman like me."

Maud completed her chores around the house and did her homework, then spent the rest of the evening making kites. She followed the instructions Andrew had given to her for making kites. Excited to be seeing her cousins soon, Maud spent her evenings after school making kites for them. She made two kites a day and ten kites by the end of week.

MamaJames was up early Saturday morning, packed a big bag with ground provisions from the garden and a change of clothes. MamaJames woke Maud and told her they were ready to go. Maud cleaned up herself, washed her face from the water-filled basin sitting on the table, and brushed her teeth using a chewstick. She then combed her hair with four big braids. "Am ready, Grandma!" she shouted.

Saint Mary borders Saint Ann, and the neighboring town to their relatives was three miles away. MamaJames rested between each mile, as her impaired leg lacked strength to keep up. They arrived an hour later than expected. Maud ran into the house with a big grin, jumping and screaming with excitement. Maud hugged her grandaunt then went outside to play with her cousins. She gave them each a kite. She was so proud of her achievement. With the grin on her face, she said boastfully, "I made them myself."

The children ran around the big yard, flying their kites. The lizards warming in the sun ran into the bushes from the children as they ran around flying their kites.

It was a hot day with a temperature of eighty-nine degrees. The trees stood still, with little to no wind. The kites didn't maintain airspeed for long. After many tries, they gave up and put their kites away.

The cousins filled the house: first, second, and third cousins from MamaJames's offsprings and some distant relatives. Most of the cousins were Maud's mother's age; others were teenagers and children. Maud's grandaunt was the baby of the eight children, and the only two surviving offspring were her and MamaJames. Maud's grandaunt went by the name Nanne to everyone.

Nanne made breakfast. She roasted several breadfruits from firewood; cooked ackee, Jamaica's most favorite dish with saltfish, tomatoes, and onions; and a big pot of chocolate tea, made with chocolate balls, spices, coconut milk, and sweetened condensed milk. The breakfast was a grand meal, reserved for big holidays. It delighted Maud and her cousins to have such a meal. "It feels like Christmastime," said Maud. The children nodded their heads in acknowledgment.

Maud asked for a second cup of chocolate tea. She liked the coconut milk cooked in the tea. Maud drank her tea, slurping. "It's so good," she remarked.

Maud spent the rest of the day playing with her cousins. The children played their favorite game: hide-and-seek.

Maud hid in the crawl space under the house. As she tried to hide, shuffling her body into the beams that held the house together, she shoveled up some earth. And buried underneath the loose dirt was a wooden doll. Maud didn't wait to be found by the hide-and-seekers. She ran into the house, holding the doll at arm's length, shouting with excitement, "Grandma, look! Look what I found!"

MamaJames grabbed the doll from Maud's arm, tears bursting from her eyes. "It's Annamay, it's your mama's!" MamaJames shouted.

Maud looked at her grandma in amazement then fixed her gaze to her grandaunt. Nanne looked back at Maud and nodded her head in acknowledgment. The discovery of Ann's wooden doll brought back memories of her daughter, and the tears flew down her cheeks as MamaJames held onto the doll. MamaJames missed her daughter dearly. Maud couldn't hold back her tears after looking into her grandma's tear-filled eyes.

Maud and her "grands" talked about Ann, her mother. The stories were wonderful, but it made Maud sad.

Maud's cousins joined in when they gave up tracking her. Some of Maud's cousins walked over and gave her a hug. Maud wiped her tears, and with a blank stare, deep in thought, she said, "I need my mother, my parents. I have to do something. Being away from my mother is driving me crazy." The thoughts engulfed her body as she distanced herself from everyone, shutting out the chatter.

Maud went to bed that night. She looked over at her family as they each took a spot on the floor of the tiny house, sleeping. They spread banana leaves on the floor, covered over with cloth, making them into beds. MamaJames, Nanne, and the smaller children slept in the bed. Maud reflected on the day's activity and smiled to herself. She had a great time and realized how much she missed her cousins.

Maud had a hard time sleeping. Her thoughts reflected on her mother and father, and she was longing to be with them. Her mother's pillow, the scent, lingered in her mind with every thought. The hair strands she pulled from the pillow were piling up. She missed the pillow while sleeping at her grandaunt's house but was happy that she had an addition to her collection of her mother's things: the wooden doll. She held the doll to her chest, feeling the connection to her mother.

Then suddenly, like a flash of lightning, the thoughts lit up in her mind. *Kites, kites! I could fly kites to communicate with my parents.* The kite-flying adventure with Andrew was an experience Maud had never seen, an experience of the wind pushing kites into the atmosphere to new places. Maud fell into a deep sleep, and the last thoughts in her mind turned into a dream.

It was a very overcast sky with clouds so thick that the sun was barely visible. Maud groaned in her sleep as the dream continued: *Her cousins and Maud let loose giant pigeons from a hilltop. The pigeons flew to her mother's house in Cuba.* Maud groaned several more times as she turned onto her side.

When the giant pigeon arrived, it swept up Mama and Papa onto its back, the pigeons flew to Jamaica, and Mama and Papa were home.

Maud awoke the next morning, not remembering much from her dream. She lay in bed, trying to process what she remembered. "Giant pigeons! Nah! Maybe kites. I could use kites to get to my parents." She searched her mind, trying to think about the depth of the dream and what it meant and came up with kite flying, not giant pigeons. She mumbled to herself, "Kites, that's it."

Maud puzzled over the distance from Jamaica to Cuba. *Could a kite go that far?* she thought.

She rolled the thoughts over and over in her mind until she believed it, believing she could do it. She mumbled, "I will make this dream into reality."

Maud got out of her bed and rounded up her cousins. She pushed them out the door, forcing them to fly kites. It was 7:00 a.m. There was a breeze, an enormous breeze. The tree branches atop the tree were dancing in the wind. With a temperature of seventy-two degrees, it was a perfect day for flying kites. Maud and her cousins each grabbed a kite and stormed into the big yard. They each took a spot on the two acres, running in the opposite direction of the dancing tree branches, with their kite behind them. The kites took off, mounting in the sky as the butterflies and birds flew away from the kites, trying to share the atmosphere. Some kites were moving faster than the others, but they all made a beautiful display.

The cousins were all shouting, "Go, kite, go" with excitement as the kites filled the atmosphere. Maud had brought an extra roll of strings, which sent her kite farther into the sky; it was so tiny, mixing in with the clouds. The cousins were all shouting with excitement when they saw Maud's kite deep into the heavens. They chanted, "Go, Maud, go!"

MamaJames and Nanne heard screaming of laughter coming from the children outside. They hurriedly made their way through the door onto the veranda. They looked up into the sky with dismay, then smiled at the beautiful display of kites in the sky.

"That's beautiful," MamaJames said to her sister.

The cousins flew their kites for hours. Maud tried to get her kite out of the sky, but it was difficult as the thirty-miles-per-hour wind fought against the kite. Maud cut the string and let her kite flow into space. The kite traveled a hundred more feet into the sky then disappeared to a new place. Maud was more convinced than ever. Kites were the way to go. After everyone had breakfast, they all sat around the house on the floor. Maud was happy with her kite-flying experience and was confident that it could bring her parents home. She approached everyone and told them of her vision, the desire to get to her parents using kites—flying the kites from Jamaica to Cuba. Laughter filled the room. Laughing was coming out from eighteen mouths. It was like a comedy show.

"Maud mission, the impossible mission," the younger children shouted. The laughter and chatter became louder as everyone added their negative thoughts. The grown-ups shouted, "It's a hideous idea."

Maud could not hear herself speak. She walked through the door outside, shutting out the insults behind her. The kites were still lying on the ground in the yard. Maud picked up the kites, held them to her chest, and said in a loud voice, "I will fly you deep into the Caribbean Sea to Cuba."

MamaJames walked to the door, feeling empathy toward her granddaughter. She could see her granddaughter kneeling on the ground, holding the kites above her head. She felt the pain and knew she had to do something.

* * *

The laughter had subsided; it was quiet when Maud walked in. She was more determined to carry out her vision. She took her stand in the middle of everyone. As she was about to speak, MamaJames shouted, interrupting her, "We will try. There's no harm in trying." She was speaking for everyone.

The cousins held their hands in the air with a smile of consent. "We all will fly kites to Cuba." The cousins' intrigued minds didn't stop there. "How will we do this?" they shouted.

The grands had an idea and wanted to add their input. They knew that the closest point from Jamaica to Cuba was in the parish of Saint James, Montego. MamaJames added, "We would have to travel there, and the wind would have to be just right blowing in the direction toward Cuba."

It perplexed Maud. With a blank stare on her face, she was soaking up in the information from her grands. She didn't think that far. Then with sparkly eyes, as if waking up from a dream, she shouted, "I got it! We can fly kites when the wind is the most powerful." She laughed in excitement. "A storm!" She continued to explain, "We will have to fly our kites during a storm or hurricane." Maud remembered reading in civic class, during a hurricane, how powerful the winds can be, and hurricanes usually affect several islands in the Caribbean. The plans were in gear. They had to make many kites and fly them in a storm.

Nanne had relatives living in Saint James: her sons and grandchildren. She hadn't seen them for a while since her grandsons became men. She chuckled with excitement. "I will see my grandchildren soon."

Maud looked around the room at her cousins and grands. The look of enthusiasm on their faces filled the room with a light of hope. Like a lamp turning up brightly, the room was suddenly lit up. She had her answer; they were all ready.

CHAPTER 4

Maud and her grandma took the journey home. The walk felt less tiresome, with each step filled with dancing and singing of excitement.

The following day after school, Maud went over to her parent's house. Andrew was working in his garden. Maud approached him and told him of her vision. He laughed at the idea at first. Maud remained steadfast and was now used to the reaction of everyone laughing. Andrew saw the pain in her face, and his reaction changed. He was ready to lend a helping hand.

"I would like to help!" he said.

Maud smiled. The pain on her face turned into joy, as she desperately needed Andrew's help. She turned to Andrew and explained the intensity to make this happen. "Am in. I will get the strong bamboo for the kites and will make as many as you want," Andrew said.

Maud smiled. She was happy. She needed all the help that she could get.

Maud needed money to make the kites, and the only thing she was good at was to plant a garden. She had worked side by side with her grandma and loved to see the product of their work.

She confided in Andrew with all her plans and perceived him as an older brother. He suggested planting callaloo. It was a fast crop taking two to three months to harvest. Andrew gave Maud some callaloo seed. Maud thanked Andrew for all his help.

Maud worked in the garden each day after school, preparing the land and planting the seeds. As she watered the garden, she noticed the callaloo plant bursting through the soil in the ground. It gave a sense of creating life and the earnestness to make her vision a reality.

* * *

It was the middle of April, and the callaloo plants were three inches out of the ground.

Andrew invited his younger brother, Amos, four years Maud's senior, to help with the making of kites. They all sat outside Maud's house under a tree that spread like an enormous umbrella, giving shade and breeze. MamaJames invited herself as they all watched Andrew show his skills of making kites using bamboo.

strings and cords used to string and fly the kites

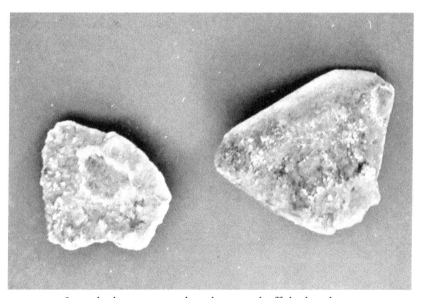

Jagged edge stone used to shave rind off the bamboos

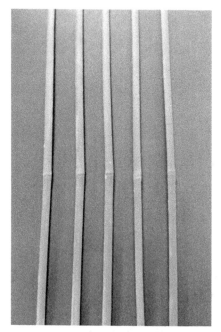

green bamboo sticks

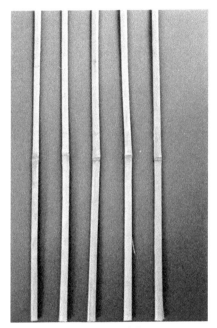

shaved, rind free

two pieces of bamboo bound together

three pieces of bamboo bound together,
making the image of a hexagon

four pieces of bamboo bound together,
making an image of a heptagon

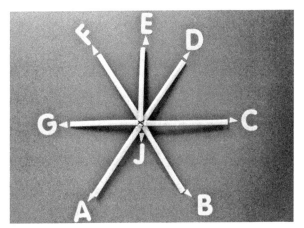

the labeling of the heptagon image

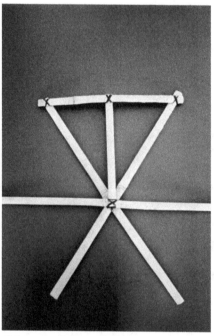

Andrew adds a small piece of bamboo from labels F to E
ending at label D to complete the frame of the kite

Stringing the frame of the kite, the cord is taken through the split in the bamboo around the circumference of the kite frame

Make the tongue of the kite, running the
cord from label F to label D

A finished kite. The arrays of beautiful colors
of the kite paper and the tail of the kite.

Andrew chose hard green bamboo for its sturdiness to sustain strong winds and its flexibility to conform to the shape of the kite, and it's easier to cut and slice in desired length. Andrew used his cutlass to cut down two bamboo trees halfway up the roots. He cut the bamboo in twenty sticks, each twelve inches long, to make four kites. Then he used a jagged-edge piece of stone as a knife to shave the green rind. He was rubbing the sharp stone vigorously against the edge of the bamboo, peeling the rinds and making it smooth. Andrew made each bamboo stick the same thickness. He then made a split one-tenth of an inch on both ends of the bamboo sticks. Andrew laid the bamboo sticks in piles of five.

He picked up two of the bamboo sticks out of a pile. He made an X with two of the bamboo sticks, using a fine piece of cord to knot them in the center. Then he added a third stick of bamboo across the X and knotted all three bamboos in the center, making an image of a hexagon. Andrew picked up one of the bamboo sticks from the pile he was using and cut it in half, making it shorter, half the size of the other bamboo sticks. Andrew then placed the bamboo stick through one triangle and knotted it in the center, making an image like a heptagon. This, he said, was the top of the kite. He labeled each bamboo in the heptagon image as: A, going left to right around the frame, B, C, D, E, F, G, and to where all the bamboo met in the center as J.

The top of the kite had four triangles, and the bottom had three triangles. To complete making the top frame of the kite, he used a shorter piece of bamboo, starting on label F, knotting the bamboo in place, then stretching the bamboo to label *E*, knotting it in place, and ending at label *D*, knotting it in place. He continued from *D* using the same cord through the split in the bamboo, taking the cord around the circumference of the frame of the kite and making a knot where he started at label *F*.

The green bamboo made the kite easier to string and conform to its new shape as the bamboo dried. To test the consistency of the cord around the circumference and the effectiveness of the bamboo, he laid the kite on a flat surface. All seven bamboo sticks should lie flat on the surface. The center *J* should be a half inch higher off the surface, making the belly of the kite. Accomplishing this image, he completed the frame of the kite.

Underneath the top of the kite, from label *F* to *D*, he ran a short piece of cord, making the tongue of the kite. He tested the consistency again, making sure the tongue and cord around the kite and the bamboo are level and sit flat on the surface.

Andrew had prepared twenty bamboo sticks in piles of five, four bamboo sticks per kite. He only used four sticks, one extra stick just in case one of the bamboo breaks when making the kite.

Andrew delegated everyone to make their kite. MamaJames went into the house to make flour into starchy paste to glue the paper to the kite frame.

MamaJames set out her ingredients to make flour paste: one cup of flour with a half cup of tap water. She poured the flour and water in a bowl, mixing until there were no lumps of flour, creating a smooth consistency. She then cooked the flour mixture on the wood fire until it was gluey. Once cool, it was ready to be applied to the kite frame.

Maud tore out pages from her writing book to cover the frame of the kites. Andrew applied the flour glue generously to the frame of the kite then covered the entire frame with paper.

He used the jagged-edge stone to cut the excessive paper then applied flour glue to the edge and sealed it over the cord and frame. He glued paper to the tongue of the kite. The tongue gave the kite style and made a buzzing sound like a queen bee when the wind blew. It took ten minutes for the paper to adhere to the frame of the kite. Once dried, Andrew demonstrated the stringing of the kite.

To string the kite, Andrew used a heavier piece of cord, starting on label F to label D, making a loop. He then poked two holes through the center J, running the cord through the center, knotting it in place around the center bamboos. He then traveled the cord to make a knot in the center of the loop, completing the stringing of the top of the kite.

To make the tail of the kite, Andrew strung a piece of cord to label A, looping to label B. Then in the center of the loop, he tied a piece of cloth two inches wide by six feet long, completing the tail of the kite. The tail of the kite can be six feet to eighteen feet long, depending on the size of the kite. The bigger the kite, the longer the tail.

The tail of the kite is very important as it propelled the kite further into the sky and is one of the most beautiful parts of the kite as it danced and whipped through the wind, as it went higher and higher into the sky. They completed their kites, strong and sturdy, but they were plain, lacking in color. Andrew commented about the white paper used to cover the kites. It was too plain. The only paper Maud had was a white paper from her schoolbook to cover the kites, and she agreed with Andrew that the kites could be more colorful.

"I have an idea," she said. "I could use wild berries and other fruits and vegetables to make dye to color the white papers."

The kite making was a big undertaking for Maud. It consumed her thoughts so much, she didn't hear when Andrew and Amos said they would help design the white paper in different colors. MamaJames observed Maud's distraction, rubbing her shoulders with her hands as if waking her up from a deep sleep.

"Oh, I'm sorry, thanks for offering." Maud was grateful for their help.

She grew up in the same district they did, eight hundred yards away, and had never interacted with them before, like the kite flying. She had always said hello in passing but had never held a conversation. With a smile on her face, she was grateful and happy. She had friends supporting her mission.

Maud's eyes drooped with exhaustion. Overwhelmed with the kite project, she was getting more distracted and could not converse with her helpers.

MamaJames saw the distraction on Maud's face as her eyes drooped and asked Andrew and his brother to leave and thanked them for helping.

The thoughts of reaching out to her parents consumed her, causing her to go deftly. Maud picked up the kites and went in the house to her bed. She took hold of her mother's pillow and held it to her chest with her head crouched down and buried into it. She took a deep breath then several more; it filled her lungs. Intoxicated, she fell asleep. Her young brain was overloaded, filled with anxiety playing out in a dream.

Mama and Papa were slaves on the plantation, bound with ropes around their waist and working in the pouring rain. The rain made a muddy mess, covering their bodies each time they fell to the ground from the slave master's beating. They looked like mummies from the mud sticking to their bodies. Their condition was unnerving. Then suddenly they heard the quacking of birds flying over their heads. Jon and Ann both looked up to the sky and saw giant birds flying over their heads, and in a flash, it swept them up. They rode onto the back of the giant ducks, rescued, and flew back to Jamaica.

Maud awoke from her dream. She thought to herself, *The same dream twice.* Smiling, she said, "This is my mission. I will replace birds with kites." She now believed that this was her mission, flying kites, and the second dream was reinforcement.

After dinner, MamaJames boiled some water on the wood fire and made a bath for Maud. It was going on her third day, one day before her regular bath day. Maud welcomed the bath. It was in MamaJames's big aluminum tub. Maud felt special. She splashed around in the big tub like a duckling. "Quack, quack, this is great," she said.

MamaJames wanted to do something special for Maud. She thought, for a child, it was a lot to undertake, and she would do anything to help her granddaughter. The key to bringing her daughter home was through her granddaughter. She had to make Maud comfortable to undertake such a task, and she was happy to do her part. She believed.

* * *

It was the weekend, a time to visit her cousins. Maud packed her kite supplies and was ready before her grandma.

Maud showed her cousins the bamboo and the steps for making the kites. She also delegated other tasks, dyeing the white papers for the kites. Maud used fruits and vegetable peels to make different colors.

For the next two months, MamaJames did most of the work around the house, leaving Maud to concentrate on the kite project.

Maud harvested her callaloo, cutting twelve stalks, then tied them in bundles. She had eleven bundles of Callaloo. Andrew sold them at the market for her. Maud made enough money to buy wool, construction cord, writing books, and fabric for the tail of the kites.

Maud needed to broaden her knowledge of storms and hurricanes from what she learned in civic class. She turned to her grandma for help.

MamaJames was in her mid-seventies; she had lived through many storms and hurricanes; she wasn't an expert but could offer her life experiences.

"The hurricane months are June to September. Hurricane comes with destructive wind and rain, so powerful it destroys houses, uproots trees—destroying everything in its path. The hurricane has an eye. The eye of the hurricane is the most peaceful part of a hurricane, and when it passes, it is the most dangerous."

Maud focused on her grandma's story then concluded that a hurricane would be more powerful than a storm. She compared the wind speed of a hurricane of over 100 miles per hour to that of a storm with less wind speed per hour.

"That could make a great impact, Grandma!" she remarked.

"That's right, it could be a catastrophe and deadly. I have seen my share of hurricanes," said MamaJames.

CHAPTER 5

It was early June 1917. Maud was out on summer break from school. She had three months before the hurricane season ended and a lot of work to complete her kite project. Maud had one more harvest of her callaloo. She put them in bundles of twelve, getting them ready for market. She cleared the field, leaving two callaloo plants for seeding. Maud saved the money from the sale of the callaloo toward their trip to Montego.

The following two weekends, Maud and her cousins worked on the kite project from 7:00 a.m. to 7:00 p.m. using the wild cherries, carrot peels, and star apples rind and other fruit rinds to make into color. They used several old food tin cans, placing the rinds and peels in separate cans, adding water, and cooking until it extracted the color from the fruits and vegetables rind. Maud then dumped each color in a dry calabash shell for cooling and thickened them into dyes. She dipped each writing paper in the calabash shell of dye. Then she used a two-inch piece of green bamboo feathered out on one end into a painting brush to spread the color evenly on each paper. They painted primary and secondary colors on the papers. The cousins pinned each paper on the clothesline to dry. Some colors on the paper ran onto other colors, causing the colors to mix, giving a rainbow effect.

Maud smiled. "The kite paper looks beautiful." She was happy with the result.

Andrew completed over five hundred green bamboo sticks. He saturated them with a little tap water to keep them from drying out before making them into kites. Maud wrote brief notes on the kite papers to her parents, from her and MamaJames. She wrote all their names on the tail of the kites, and on the tongue of the kites, she wrote kiss symbols: *xx*.

Maud divided the workload between her home and her grandaunt's. All together they had completed 85 kites. Ten of the kites were over 3 feet tall, twenty were 2 feet, and the rest were 1 foot. The three feet kites needed strength and power to fly and were for the adults, or persons who were 66 inches tall and weighed over 150 pounds. They also needed a heavier cord, a longer tail, and a place the length of half a soccer field to launch. The 3 feet kites would go deeper in the sky and travel hundreds of miles. Maud held the kite to her body. It was up past her waist. She was happy with the prospects of the big kite. With a broad smile, it convinced her that the big kites would make it to the shores of Cuba.

* * *

It was now the middle of July. The temperature soared most days to ninety-eight degrees—no rain, dry, and hot. The leaves on the tree and the grass on the ground were brown, reflecting the humid dry weather. The grass was so parched from the weather it crunched when walked on. Maud remembered her grandma telling her when it's this hot, there was a storm or hurricane out in the sea.

Nanne's son Paul lived and worked at an old slave estate plantation in Montego along with his family. Paul's great-grandfather and grandfather were drivers on the slave plantation. Their work ethic was outstanding, and the master considered them some of the most valuable workers on the estate. After slavery ended in the nineteenth century, the master posted land for sale on the plantation to the workers. Paul's grandfather got the first opportunity to buy land because of his lineage loyalty.

The master needed help on the plantation and included a legal clause to the buyers to stay and work on the plantation until they completed the mortgage. Paul's grandfather bought three acres of land and built a house for him and his family. His grandfather's honesty and reliability gave his offspring the advantage for jobs on the plantation.

The Spice Estate was over eight hundred acres of land. The great house had six bedrooms, an enormous dining room (used for meals and meetings), two bathrooms, and a gigantic kitchen. It was a vast house built on a hill. Paul and his sons lived and worked on the plantation. Their job duties were taking care of the grounds, cutting the grass, attending to the garden, and harvesting the spice grown on the plantation. Paul inherited the three acres passed down to him by his grandfather. Paul lived in a two-bedroom house with his wife and his youngest son. His older son lived in his grandfather's house next door to Paul's house. Paul built a bigger house, after paying off the sixty years' mortgage note. He gave his older son and family his grandfather's house.

Nanne wrote a letter to her son Paul, about the kite project and wanting somewhere to stay. She dictated the letter to her older granddaughter living with her, as she couldn't read or write. Nanne received a reply five weeks later.

Paul wrote in his reply that he would love to accommodate them, but they would have to work on the plantation in exchange for staying with him.

It was September 10, twenty days before the hurricane season ended. It would take Maud and the kite crew two to three days to travel by a mule-driven cart from Saint Ann to Saint James. MamaJames paid for the transportation, using some money Maud got from her last crop of the callaloo. She arranged two mule-driven carts, which she rented from Andrew's father. Maud, Andrew, and Amos packed the cart with forty kites, food, clothes, and Maud's mother's pillow. Maud and her grandma sat in the cart driven by Andrew. Amos followed in the other cart. The crew set out on the three-mile trip to Saint Ann to pick up Nanne and her cousins.

They arrived in Saint Ann forty-five minutes later. Nanne and her family clapped their hands in excitement as the carts entered the yard. They quickly loaded the carts with the other kites, food, and their clothes. They dispersed themselves into the carts, following Andrew's directions of three adults and four children to each cart. The other young adults walked alongside the carts. Andrew divided the group based on their weight so it wouldn't be too much for the mule to pull. MamaJames asked for deliverance before taking off on their journey. Everyone held hands as she prayed to God for a safe trip and the kite mission a success. Andrew tugged on the reins to the mules. "Gallop, gallop," he said.

They set out on their trip at 7:00 a.m. with twenty-two people—enough for a soccer team.

MamaJames started humming. Her sister Nanne joined in as they sang different church songs. It was a joyful sound, breaking the monotony of the mule's galloping. After four hours of travel, they stopped under a tree by the side of the road for lunch. The children fed the mules water and vegetables.

As they continued on their journey, it became unbearably hot. The perspiration ran down their backs, soaking their clothes; it felt like the sun was immediately over their heads. The blazing heat from the sun forced them to stop for shade. They poured water over their heads to stay cool then wrapped their heads with dhuku, an Africa head wrap. The children sponged the mule's faces with water to keep them cool and brushed their body, stimulating the muscles.

The kite crew made little mileage because of the scorching heat, which halted their first day trip shorter than planned.

They arrived at Nanne's daughter's house in Trelawny at 7:00 p.m. They disembarked from the carts. Nanne's daughter Cherry welcomed them in her home. They were all sweaty, and the dust from the earth stuck to their faces and clothes, causing an unpleasant odor. Cherry pulled her blouse from her neck, covering her nose. She pulled her mother and aunt to the side, away from everyone, as she gasped for breath, whispering in their ears, "They musty! I can't have them staying in my house. They all need a bath."

Cherry suggested going to Rio Bueno to bathe.

Nanne agreed. She too was hot and sticky from the blazing heat of the sun, and the dust kicked up by the mules covered her body like a thick layer of clay. Cherry lived a half mile from the stream leading to the Rio Bueno River.

Nanne got everyone's attention. "Silence!" Her voice was loud and filled with authority, like a judge in a courtroom. "We are going to Rio Bueno River for a family outing," she screamed at the top of her lungs.

The reaction was electrifying. Everyone was shouting in agreement as they ran to the river. Its path was paved with big river rock-like steps. They leaped from one rock to another like frogs. The group jumped in the Rio Bueno River with their clothes on. Big and small trees caressed the bank of the river and its surroundings, giving the river shade and beauty.

Maud shouted, "This is paradise." The water was warm like a mineral bath. The tiny ripples of the water splashed on their bodies, cleansing and healing their sore muscles. Fatigue fell on everyone after swimming. The adult males slept in the carts under a tree. It was a tight squeeze for the others, sleeping on the floor in the house. Maud fell asleep right away, wrapping her legs and arms around her mother's pillow, breathing her mother's scent to a deep sleep.

* * *

MamaJames and her sister prepared breakfast. They were up at 3:30 a.m. Everyone got ready after eating and reloaded the carts. Hanging their wet clothes on the side of the cart to dry, they set out on their journey. Cherry and her family joined the kite crew, walking alongside the carts with their grown-up children. MamaJames started with a whistle then a tune, a usual thing she did when there was a group of people to listen to her singing. Maud put her palm in the air, stopping her grandma in her tracks. "Wait, Grandma, wait! We need a name," she shouted. "The Kites of Love. We should call ourselves The Kites of Love."

There were clapping and smiles of approval from the crew. "That's an illustrious name," cried MamaJames. "Let's pray on this."

MamaJames prayed, thanking God for their title and hope for deliverance. They all chanted, "The Kites of Love will bring us deliverance. We pray to you, O God. The Kites of Love will bring us deliverance. We pray to you, O God."

They chanted these verses several more times until MamaJames changed the song. It was another joyous moment as she sang; it felt like church.

Then suddenly, Andrew saw two big dogs running toward them. The dogs were let loose by their owners: two young White men. The mules raised their legs in defense as the dogs approached, shoving everyone to the back of the cart. Fearing for their safety, everyone jumped out of the cart except for the grands. They were too old to undertake such action. MamaJames and Nanne cried in agony, holding on to their backs, which were sore from the tilting of the cart when the mules reacted to the dogs' attack. They sat in the cart shivering in fear for their life.

MamaJames and Nanne were born into slavery. The mistreatment and cruelty by the hands of their master toward their families brought back terrible memories.

As the two White men ran behind the dogs, their insane laughter became louder and evil spit came from their mouths. They commanded the dogs to attack. "Sic 'em, sic 'em! The niggers in the cart are going to market for sale," shouted the men.

The Kites of Love children hid behind the cart, crying and fearing for their lives. The Kites of Love men walked to the front of the cart to hold their ground. Andrew spoke up, fearing that they might hurt the mules. He stood between the carts, holding both reins. His voice cracked as he tried to talk. "Don't hurt the mules! Leave us alone." He was sweating profusely from fear and anger. The dogs jumped onto Andrew, knocking him to the ground, as the White men commanded the dogs to sic 'em.

The grands stood in the cart, watching the attack. They immediately threw out some food at the dogs to distract them from causing more harm to Andrew. The dogs let go of Andrew's arm and chased the food. Thanks to the quick thinking of the grands, Andrew sustained a few paw scratches on his arms. His long-sleeved shirt protected him and his dhuku head tie.

The taller of the two White men jumped on Andrew and slapped him several times in the face as he shouted with rage, "Don't hit my dogs, you bastards!"

The children looked on, crying their eyes out. The crying became louder. "Don't kill him!" they shouted. The plea from the children touched the White men.

The attackers kicked Andrew in his stomach as they retreated then grabbed hold of their dogs. "We don't want your stinky food." The men laughed as they ran down the street in the opposite direction.

Slavery ended, but the African descendants were still in bondage and treated inferior to the White settlers, fearing for their lives every time the two races came in contact. Andrew was in shock. His breathing was heavy and was crying uncontrollably like having a fit. The Kites of Love men helped him into the cart.

Nanne and MamaJames cleaned Andrew's wounds and applied some herbal medicine to the dog scratches. Andrew could not coach the cart. MamaJames advised him to take it easy and just be a passenger. Cherry's husband took the reins and coached the cart to Montego. The young men and some children walked alongside the cart to give Andrew room to rest and heal. The attack shocked everyone. They were in silence for many miles; it broke their spirit. The children expressed their sadness and hatred for the action of the transgressors. They regained some peace as they gazed into the distance ahead, filled with rainbows of butterflies and wildflowers.

The clothes they hung on the cart to dry were now damp. As the sun heated to boiling point, they used the damp clothes to cover their necks and heads to stay cool. The Kites of Love arrived in Montego at 8:00 p.m. They were happy to be at Paul's house, and as they pulled into the yard, they sang, "We shall overcome someday, deep in my heart I do believe, we shall overcome someday."

CHAPTER 6

The magnitude of the group amazed Paul. His face showed astonishment as he tried to speak—there was a laugh then a stutter of words. "We-el…welcome, Mom. Welcome, everyone."

He hugged his mom as she disembarked from the cart and greeted the other twenty-seven family and friends. *How the hell am I going to house all these people?* he thought, staring at the large group.

Nanne didn't tell her son how many people were coming, as she didn't know herself. She was happy to take part, believing in her niece and the willingness to help her sister.

Paul, with a perplexed look on his face, was filled with anguish. *I don't have enough room to house everyone.* His thoughts stretched from one corner of his brain to the next. His anguish turned into sympathy. *They look tired from trav-*

eling. Don't be so mean. He answered himself, *I will have to give them a place to stay and a warm meal.*

Paul and his wife made dinner for the crew: white rice, callaloo, and lemonade. The Kites of Love sat around the wood fire eating dinner.

Paul had to figure out how to accommodate everyone. He asked his sons to accompany him on a walk to discuss their accommodation. He needed to confide in the family, his sons. They sat under a gigantic tree away from the house, throwing out ideas. "The two houses aren't big enough to house everyone," he said to his sons.

Paul's empathy was short-lived. He was not happy that they packed his house like sardines in a can.

"Boy, get me some tea!" he demanded his younger son to make him a can of tea on the fire.

His older son, Moses, saw his demeanor changed and the way he spoke to his younger brother. "Don't talk like that, Father. You're not a driver!"

"That's it!" The thoughts came from his son's mouth gave him the idea. "Driver and slave and slaves' quarters." "Oh, that's a brilliant thought." Paul embraced his son in approval.

"I can house everyone in the old slave quarters, on the Spice Estate, the harvest house." Paul was the overseer of the estate, the foreman in charge of the twenty workers. As a foreman, he was in charge and felt privileged to do whatever he wanted. So at 3:30 a.m., Paul moved everyone to the harvest house.

Maud and the other members of The Kites of Love followed Paul to the harvest house. Half asleep, they looked like zombies. Their steps were wobbly, having little control over their body, drugged as if overdosed by herbal medication. They wrapped their bodies in their sleeping covers to shield from the dew. The light from the heavens broke the darkness.

As the moon shone its light onto their path, they followed the voice of Paul as he led the way to the harvest house. Exhausted from walking, they crashed on the floor of the harvest house, sleeping.

The sound of a ringing bell awoke them as Paul shouted, "Get up, everyone, wake up."

Maud opened her eyes. It felt like she was sleeping for five minutes. Grumpily, she said, "We just went to sleep."

Paul was standing in the middle of the house.

Maud wiped her eyes, getting the sleep out. The sun was rising; she examined her surroundings.

The harvest house was an enormous barn with two levels. Paul gave everyone a quick history of the estate. Maud sat on the floor and took it all in. The harvest house was labeled "HS" and adjoined to the slaves' quarters, renamed the mechanical house (MH).

After slavery ended, the master changed the slaves' quarters, conforming it into a storage shed, storing his farm machineries and equipment. These farm machineries replaced the human resources of the slaves.

The harvest house was used to store banana crops and prepare cinnamon. The loft stored the ready product, boxed, bottled, and ready for export. The windows in the loft were enormous. Windows the size of doors brought light into the building. There were two staircases on either side of the building for easy access to bring and take out products. The staircases were long, twenty-four steps, and lacked handrailings. The workers developed a technique by accessing the stairs by using their back against the wall as an anchor going up and down the stairs with heavy load.

There were twenty gigantic beams that held the building in place. Down stairs had four big farm doors for lighting and to bring the horse cart in and out of the house for loading and unloading. The walls were painted white to give light to the house and for writing tasks for the workers. Paul wrote these instructions in charcoal daily, as tasks change every day.

Maud shouted out, "Could we use the tables for sleeping?"

Paul continued to talk, ignoring Maud's request. There were dozens of tables covered with huge khaki textured cloth used for laying out the spices. Stacks of straw baskets were pile alongside the walls and under the tables used for carrying products to different locations.

Straws stacked in piles alongside the walls of the harvest house were used to cover the bananas for ripening and as a cushion for export of other products.

The unique scent of cinnamon filled the harvest house, and as the air outside bellowed in the aroma became stronger.

"I could live here forever. The cinnamon smell is so good," Maud remarked.

Her chest moved up and down as she took many deep breaths, filling her lungs with the cinnamon scent. Maud couldn't get enough as she rolled around on the floor in the barn, hoping to get the scent on her clothes.

Paul ordered everyone to stay in the harvest house during the day, afraid the master might see them. Maud and The Kites of Love followed Paul in the mechanical house. Maud looked at all the machineries, horses, and carts. She had never seen such things before. Paul concluded the history of the Spice Estate. He informed the men to sleep in the harvest house, the females and children sleep in the mechanical house, and his mother and aunt in his house.

The harvest house was around a thousand feet from the great house. The master never visited unless there was a problem with the harvest yield. It worried Paul that the master would find out his family was staying at the harvest house.

Paul had to act with caution and be careful that the master never visited the harvest house during the time his family was staying. The master trusted Paul with everything; he was the foreman in charge of overseeing the plantation and the communicator between him and the operation of the estate. Everything that happened on the estate was documented and reported once weekly in a written report and monthly in the great house at a roundtable meeting, over Blue Mountain coffee. Paul was not about to tell his master of his relatives staying on the property. His weekly report was due soon, and the monthly report was due in two weeks. Paul was confident that his family would leave before the end of the month. "I really don't want to lie," Paul mumbled to himself

Maud saw the way Paul conducted himself; he commanded authority. She called her cousin Uncle Paul instead of just Paul to give him that respect. It made her feel good.

Paul welcomed his family to the harvest house and extended happiness to have them.

The family traveled from Saint Ann to Paul's house in Saint James because of the strategic point to Cuba, hoping their kites from Jamaica would reach the shores of Cuba. Paul thought to himself that the gathering of this magnitude of his family at the harvest house wasn't as important as a funeral or a wedding. These occasions are self-explanatory and wouldn't need the master's approval. The magnitude of his family gathering for kite flying was less important. It burdened Paul; he felt it didn't warrant any importance, of the master's approval, and if his master found out, this could destroy the trust and maybe his job.

Maud could see the load on Paul's shoulders, the burden and the responsibility to accommodate everyone and keep it a secret from his master. His shoulders hunched from trying to keep his head in place. Three inches shorter, he looked like a ailing old man. She felt empathy toward him, but she had a mission to complete: fly her kites. Maud thought to herself, *Am I being selfish?*

She shouted, "I will do my best to be careful and do as you say, Uncle Paul."

"That's right, Maud," he replied.

Paul satisfied his worried thoughts. *It is what it is, and it's too late to turn back.* With a more content self, he smiled and walked over to his mama. He hugged her and gave God the glory for having her here with him.

"Where is your brother Samuel?" Nanne asked.

Paul replied, "I don't know." His eyes blinked several times.

Maud looked up at her uncle, and she knew he lied. He hugged and kissed his sisters and their family. He gave the same praise to his aunt MamaJames. Then he turned his gaze on Maud with sparkling eyes of satisfaction. He was proud of her achievements. As he hugged her, he said, "An eleven-year-old putting on such a project, The Kites of Love!" He gave her a big kiss on her cheek.

"Thank you, Uncle Paul, and thanks for having us," Maud said.

There were over thirty family members, including Andrew and Amos. Paul continued to execute his plans, giving instructions to everyone, children and adults, to work in the harvest house. Dinner and breakfast were at his house. Paul hoped, with the extra human resources, he could accomplish a lot, making his master happy.

They stored the kites in the loft of the harvest house, in small, medium, and large. Andrew instructed The Kites of Love that the large kites were for the adult males, as it needed strength and knowledge to fly, while the medium-sized kites were for young adults, and the small kites were for the children. There were eighty-five kites.

Maud added her two pennies to the conversation. "The adults and grown-ups should grab two kites when it is time." These instructions made it easier for everyone to grab and go when the hurricane hits.

It had been almost a week since everyone arrived. They worked in the harvest house and ended each day with dinner at Paul's house.

CHAPTER 7

Grandma and Nanne were up one morning, earlier before everyone. They started the wood fire for breakfast. As they gathered wood for the fire, they heard a loud chirping sound.

"Did you hear that?" Nanne said.

The sisters both looked up into the heavens and noticed that there were several flocks of birds flying to the north of the island. This was a sign that something terrible was coming their way; the birds sensed the different pressure in the atmosphere and would flow away to safety. As the dawn left the sky, there was a dusky look on the atmosphere. It covered the sun over with a thick gray cloud. Grandma and Nanne predicted that there was rain, or worse, a storm in the forecast. The two ladies finished making breakfast and invited everyone by the fire.

They all gathered in the back of the house, sitting on rocks, tree leaves, and on whatever they could find. Nanne gazed up to the heavens and instructed everyone to do the same.

"It's dark!" cried the children.

Maud repeated, "It's very dark, Nanne. Is it going to rain?"

Paul, Nanne, and MamaJames stood in the circle of everyone.

Paul addressed the family. "This could be just rain or a hurricane coming our way. It's been boiling hot the last three weeks, and with the sky this dark, we are going to get something."

Maud shouted, "This could be the hurricane that's coming."

Grandma smiled and said, "Yes, child."

Paul set in place tasks for everyone to do to prepare for the storm or hurricane. The ladies cooked goat and pork meat on the wood fire stove, roasting these to a crisp crust, to preserve the meat for days. The children picked carrots, corn, and other vegetables from the garden. Everybody chipped in gathering firewood, getting water from the well, and filling wash pans for cooking and drinking. They stored some food and water in the harvest house, just in case Paul's house didn't hold up in the storm. Built like a fortress, the harvest house could withstand strong winds and had seen many hurricanes. Paul gathered the group and led them to the highest point of the property where the kites would be launched. Maud walked along with the group. The air got thinner as she walked up the slope; the ground was filled with dry leaves and broken branches, which crunched under her feet with every step. Maud looked around at her surroundings. Tree branches spread over one another, intertwined with other branches. It made the atmosphere darker with the already overcast sky. It was a long walk to the launch site. Maud was getting impatient. She thought to herself, *There is no way we can launch our kites here.*

"Come on, Maud, let's go!" Grandma shouted. It was a break in Maud's thoughts as MamaJames called out to her. Maud looked ahead at the group. She was at least five hundred yards behind everyone. Maud ran up the hill to catch up. She was breathing fast and deep, then she lost her breath as she looked at the kites' launch site. It took her breath away. She held onto her knees to catch her breath. As her lungs expanded, she shouted, "Oh my...oh my god! This is perfect." With a big smile on her face, she was happy. She glanced over to The Kites of Love group. They possessed the same reaction: a big contagious smile. It satisfied them.

It was a lookout cliff with an area the size of a soccer field. The land was bare, with trees off to the side, completed by a beautifully manicured lawn. The sea was down below, and as far as the eyes could see, there was the blue water of the ocean. Tree stumps were all over for seating, giving a beautiful display to the lookout cliff.

Maud and the other children jumped with joy, masquerading with excitement. Grandma did her thing, chanting, "The Kites of Love will bring us deliverance, we pray to you, O God."

Everyone joined in dancing and singing. They masqueraded with their hands in the air while some men took their shirts off, waving them over their heads and dancing. It was a revival, like a church on Mount Olive. Maud named the lookout cliff Deliverance. She stabbed a tree limb deep into the ground. So did everyone, claiming the land. The dancing went on for hours as they descended Deliverance.

The Kites of Love congregated at Uncle Paul's house. He went over the last-minute plans for The Kites of Love. Everyone agreed with the plans and knew what their tasks were.

Maud shouted, "Hip, hip, hurray. Are you all ready!"

The Kites of Love shouted back, "Yes, we are!" It was like a sporting match; they were all ready to beat their opponent and be victorious.

Maud shouted "Victory!" making sure everyone felt the good vibes, and victory was now a part of their soul.

Uncle Paul and his sons battened down the windows with aluminum zinc and cleared the yard free of any obstacle that might prevent the floodwater from flowing freely. The men and women went to the harvest house, working and getting ready for the storm, stocking produce in the loft and securing the windows with aluminum zincs. Maud and the other children stayed with the grands, roasting more food for what's to come, a storm or hurricane.

* * *

It was September 19. Grandma and Nanne went outside to make breakfast. As they opened the door to the outside, they could feel the high wind on their faces. Simultaneously they looked up to heavens. The sky was black, with clouds hanging just above the trees. The trees went crazy in the wind as the branches gave off sprinkling of raindrops deposited on the leaves that poured on their heads. The grands made breakfast, covering the food with big green banana leaves to keep the rain and wind out.

After breakfast, everyone went to the harvest house, taking more food and clothes. Uncle Paul ordered the adults to stay busy at work. He inherited good work ethic from his great-grandfather. The children got off scot-free and used their time to play games. Maud and her cousins sat on the ground in a circle, like at a camp. When Maud looked closer at the ground beneath her feet, she noticed many cone-shaped holes beneath the earth. She put her finger into the holes to see what made such a beautiful sculpture on the ground. The cone-shaped hole caved in, filling the hole with more earth, becoming a flat surface. One of Maud's younger cousins poked her finger in another cone-shaped hole in the ground and started singing, "Nanny, Nanny, come for your rice and peas. If you don't come, Mama and Papa will eat it off." She sang the chorus several more times until a tiny ant-like insect emerged from the ground.

Nanne walked over to where the children were playing and saw the ant lions that they had caught in an old can. Maud asked her grandaunt what animals they were.

Nanne explained to Maud and the other children, "These insects live in shallow sand in the ground, making a funnel shape by backing into the sand, forming a pit to trap other tiny insects. They are from the lacewing group of insects, also known as ant lions. When you put your finger in the cone-shaped holes in the ground using several circular motions or poked as if drilling, an ant lion will appear to the surface. Singing doesn't bring them out of their hole, but it makes the action fun."

Maud was excited to gain the knowledge. She mimicked her cousin, poking the hole with her finger in a circular motion while singing, "Nanny, Nanny, come for you rice and peas. If you don't come, Mama and Papa will eat it off."

Maud was so excited to see the ant lions come to the surface of the earth. She chuckled. "It was so much fun." She caught several more of ant lion, putting them in an old can.

* * *

Only a handful of workers showed up for work on the Spice Estate. *It might be because of the terrible weather*, Paul thought.

The older children were used to filling in the shortage of workers. Paul was happy that he was a week early off his work schedule. His master would be pleased.

* * *

74

The big giant door swung open with a bang as the wind pushed it, causing it to slam hard against the wall. The master walked in. He never visited the harvest house, but today he did. The master came to the harvest house to check on his investment and the coming hurricane. He shouted, "Paul! Paul, where are you?" It was hard to see Paul over The Kites of Love crew.

Paul held his hand up. "Here I am, Master Graham!"

Uncle Paul walked toward his master. Maud stood to her feet when she heard the master's voice.

Master Graham, a White man of British descent, stood seventy-eight inches tall, with broad shoulders, receding hairline with a mixture of gray and blond hair, and long sideburns growing into his beard. He stood with authority.

Uncle Paul acknowledged, "Master, Master, here I am." He bowed several times, as if bowing to the king of England. He retreated a little, stepping backward, giving respect to his master.

"Why are all these children and people here? I want everyone out of here!" The master was furious as he pointed his index finger in a rage.

Paul had never questioned his master, but today, he tried to explain about his family staying.

"I don't want to hear your lame excuse," the master said. With eyes fixed on Paul, he didn't acknowledge anyone else in the house. The master continued, "Get everything ready. A hurricane is coming!"

He babbled on, repeating himself, "A hurricane is coming our way, and I want everything packed away and stored to the loft level."

Paul was ahead of his schedule, and he secured the product and did everything to prepare for the hurricane. The master didn't take the time to look at the progress Paul had made; instead, he spent his energy, his pent-up energy, on the people on his property.

Maud fixed her stare on Master Graham. She had never seen a White master this close. She turned to her grandma and whispered, "He's a mean giant."

The Kites of Love left immediately as the master commanded. The wind was now climbing at a speed of forty miles an hour. The grands and the smaller children had difficulty walking, falling to the ground like a stumbling block as the strong wind toppled them over. Like troopers, they didn't let the wind beat them down. They were crawling on their hands and knees back to Paul's house.

The master's action embarrassed Paul in front of his family. He hung his head like an inferior animal, pacing back and forth in the harvest house, trying to grow back into a man.

Paul was determined to let his feelings known. As he shivered, afraid of the consequence, he mumbled under his breath, "This could cost me my job, maybe even losing our house." He uttered aloud, "The Kites of Love must go on!" His determination took on a fresh approach. He shouted with pain of emotions, "The kite flying is a justifiably, and it will prevail." He didn't care if the master approved.

The master pulled the door open with a force, causing it to hit hard against the wall as he walked out.

The handful of workers that showed up stayed. It could be very difficult with the wind speed climbing for them to walk two or more miles to their homes in this weather.

The workers were astonished to see Master Graham walking in the harvest house but was happy that Paul stood up to him. Paul thanked the workers that showed up. They respected and looked up to him as their foreman.

* * *

It was 5:00 p.m., dinnertime. The workers followed Paul to his house. The wind howled like a dog, picking tree branches in its path, crashing against their body as they trotted to the house. Paul dug up the cooked food he buried in the ground of his house. He stored the cooked food in a hole into the ground to keep it cool and prevent it from spoiling. The grands shared the food cold as it was impossible to fire up the wood fire in the rain and wind.

The houses were used to spread out the family and the ten workers who stayed back to help. Paul introduced the workers to Maud. "This is the person who brought everyone together, The Kites of Love inventor."

Maud waved hello and thanked them for helping.

Uncle Paul was determined to see the kite project through, having an interest of his own. His hands were now tied, and he had to do what was best for everyone even if it meant going against the master's orders. Paul instructed everyone to meet at the harvest house at midnight. It would accommodate everyone, plus it was closer to the lookout cliff and already stocked with the kite supplies. Paul's prediction for the hurricane: the wind speed would increase ten to twenty miles an hour by midnight. Uncle Paul used a small windmill-like object he planted into the ground outside the back door of his house, which he used to measure the wind speed.

The wind was howling like a mad dog outside, and the speed of the wind had increased. The tree branches went crazy. Paul appointed two of his workers to keep watch. He needed visuals from his windmill and any large flying debris to determine the intensity of the hurricane and if he needed to move everyone to the harvest house sooner.

Paul went to bed and informed everyone to do the same. "We should rest and be ready for the hurricane."

The houses were crowded. They occupied every place on the floor, sleeping and looking like mummies wrapped up in their sheets.

* * *

It was 11:40 p.m. The workers woke Paul and informed him of large flying debris and the windmill spinning out of control. Paul gathered everyone in his house then went over to his son's and got everyone up. They covered their heads with ragged clothes and sheltered their bodies from the rain with banana leaves. The wind and rain were whipping and piercing everything in sight, as if fighting to claim victory. They used kerosene lanterns to guide the way, running as fast as they could to the harvest house. The Kites of Love crew had gotten bigger with over thirty-three family members, Maud's neighbors, and the ten workers.

Nanne's leg swung out from underneath as the strong wind pushed her to the ground. Paul was helping his mom to her feet when he stepped on a tree branch and fell on top of her. The children saw an opportunity to have some fun: jumping onto Paul's back. Others joined in the fun, jumping on one another, like a football game fighting to win the ball. It was a wet battle. Everyone rolled around in the rain and wind. It was a joyful moment as the family united in the harmony of pre-hurricane.

CHAPTER 8

September 20, a little after midnight, everyone arrived at the harvest house.

Master Graham was looking through his window, watching the storm, when he saw a light moving toward the harvest house. Curiosity was getting the better of him. Master Graham put his raincoat on and grabbed his shotgun, prepared to stop whatever was moving toward the harvest house. As he walked, a rush of rain showers forced him to take shelter underneath a gigantic oak tree. Shortly after, the wind picked up with a mighty force, tossing the oak tree branches filled with a multitude of raindrops, showering down onto Master Graham. The thunder roared and the lightning flashed. Master Graham tried to run away from under the oak tree when he tripped over a broken tree branch, and he fell to the ground. Master Graham cried out for help, but the wind was howling, making his cry for help like the sound of a whisper. He tried to get up but could not walk. Master Graham hurt his leg when he fell. Determined to get out of the storm to safety, he crawled on his hands and good leg in the direction of the harvest house.

The grands and the children changed into dry clothes. The others kept on their rain-filled clothes as they knew that they would be back in the rain flying their kites. The workers took turns checking the status of the hurricane, periodically looking through a tiny crack in the door, when they noticed something moving in the wind. The moving object caught their attention; they opened the door wider to get a good look. The lightning flashes illuminated the outside, bringing to light a pale object dangling as the atmosphere went from light to dark. The workers went back inside to alert everyone as to what they saw. Paul and the workers went outside with their lanterns. They combed the grounds in the directions to where the image was spotted. As they approached, they saw the image of a hand waving, the body faced down, and a whisper coming out, "Help…help me! I have been hit by lightning." The mighty wind blew the sound toward them.

"It's Master…Master Graham!" Paul recognized the voice. He ran fast to rescue his master. He flipped the master over to his back. "What the hell? What are you doing out in the hurricane?" Paul said frantically. The men anchored the master inside the harvest house. They lay him on one work-table and covered him with several tablecloths. The layers of cloth warmed his body as he trembled from the rain-filled clothes that stuck to his body. The men massaged the master's leg, rubbing it vigorously to get the blood flowing, and poured some warm kerosene oil from the lantern for a deeper massage.

Master Graham refused dry clothes when Paul offered. "I am fine," he barked back. Master Graham thought to himself, *I would be dead before I wear a Negro's clothes.* Master Graham was furious when the Black people touched him, massaging his leg. He shut his eyes in anguish, not looking at them as they put their soul in making him better. He wanted to stop them, but he needed help and would take it from anyone.

Maud saw the change in Master Graham's face. She felt sorry for him. She shared her thoughts of Master Graham with her grandma. "How can someone be so selfish? We are helping, not inflicting pain."

"That's how men are. They feel that they are God's greatest creation and therefore are superior to all." MamaJames continued, "And being the master, he will never heed to others."

Maud brought the master some water. She ignored his ignorance and filled it with kindness. "He is human like us and needed help," she mumbled under her breath. Maud braced herself for the worst, just in case he refused the water.

The master rested after drinking the water then got up from the table into a sitting position. His legs dangled under the table from his tall stature. Maud and the others gathered around to see if the master was fine. The master looked to his left then to the right, his eyes scanning the house, searching for Paul. He didn't acknowledge anyone else. His stare was filled with complexity.

Maud looked at the giant man sitting on the table. His hair was dripping wet and filled with leaves, debris stuck to his hair and face from falling in the storm. The master inched himself off the table into a crouch position. He clenched his fist in anger. His facial features changed. With furrowed eyebrows, he looked mad, furious.

Maud retreated and took a few steps back away from the master. She was afraid—afraid of what the master might do.

The master locked his eyes with Paul, waiting for an answer, an explanation to why all these people were still in the harvest house. The master's stare was deadly, like a superior animal protecting his territory. He needed an answer right now.

Paul looked to the left then to his right, mimicking his master. He pulled Maud close to him, clutching her under his arm. "These are my family!" he shouted. He continued, "We are The Kites of Love."

"What is that?" the master asked as he stood upright. He had regained his strength, and his voice roared like thunder in the room. "Get out!" he shouted.

Master Graham was furious with Paul for defying his orders and reminded him that he was in charge. He reinforced his demands, "You all need to leave right now!"

Paul broke his bind with Maud. He took two steps facing his master; he was ready to fight for his family, The Kites of Love crew, and, at whatever cost, maybe lose his job. He believed in his cousin's mission and his own interest in finding his brother. Paul opened his mouth to reply to his master when the thunderclaps drowned out his voice. The master jumped in fear at the sudden sound of thunder.

"Ha!" Maud uttered with a sigh of relief, saved by the thunder.

She murmured, "Thank God." It terrified her of the outcome. Her fear was that Uncle Paul could be fired for his insubordination.

Maud and her cousins laughed at the master's reaction to the thunder.

The lightning flashed several more times, like sharp waves of sunlight coming through the windows.

Paul reversed his steps and walked away from his master, toward the door. As he opened the door, it slammed open, hitting against the wooden wall. A rush of wind bellowed inside. The wind had picked up to ninety miles per hour. The hurricane was here.

Master Graham dried his wet hair with the table covering and tucked his shirt in his pants. Composing himself, he showed his authority.

Maud didn't take her eyes off the master. She was worried that he might stop the kite mission. So she incited her cousins to sing, sing loudly, hoping her strategy would drown out his voice if he tried to throw them out again. The hurricane was now in high gear, over one hundred miles per hour wind speed. It was obvious that no one could leave. They were all prisoners, even Master Graham.

Paul avoided contact with his master. Instead, he concentrated on the hurricane. Master Graham couldn't leave to check on his family. He sat on top of the table. He murmured, "They outnumbered me. I am the minority." For the first time, Master Graham was not in control. He glanced over at the group singing and realized that Maud was the conductor. She was in control.

He mumbled, "Maud, a child in an adult's body, she was in charge."

Paul opened the door every hour, checking on the eye of the hurricane, and instructed everyone, adults and children, to prepare to leave during the eye of the hurricane.

Maud grabbed hold of her mother's pillow and took a big swift "I love you, Ma, hope to see you soon."

It was 3:00 a.m.; the hurricane wind speed peaked at 110 miles per hour. The sound of debris hitting against the harvest house, mixed with rain and wind, sounded like a thousand horses on a rabbit chase. The raging sound of the hurricane went on for hours. Then suddenly it stopped.

Paul shouted, "The eye of the hurricane is here, let's go!" Everyone ran to the loft to grab a kite. Paul led the pack, running as fast as he could. Immediately behind him was Maud. They arrived at Deliverance. Out of breath running, they looked at one another, filled with excitement. The grin on their faces lit up the atmosphere. They shouted, "The moment had finally arrived." They had twenty to thirty minutes to launch and fly their kites before the eye of the hurricane passed.

MamaJames led the group in prayer, praying to God for a miracle. "Amen!" the group shouted. They chanted, "Deliverance, deliverance," as they all got busy getting their kites in the air. They launched half of the kites in the air in five minutes, in the eastern direction, toward Cuba. The grands couldn't get their kites off the ground. Maud ran with the kite behind her. The wind picked up the kite from the ground; she gave the kite string several tugs and then fed it more strings as the kite flew to the air. MamaJames took the kite string from her granddaughter. "Thanks, Maud." MamaJames watched as her kite flew deeper and deeper to the sky. With a big smile on her face, she said, "Yes! Go, kite, go!"

The men, Paul, Andrew, Amos, and the workers, flew the big kites. Once the first set of kites reached the desired altitude, they tied the kite strings to the tree stumps to keep them in place before releasing. Maud and her cousins flew a second kite. There was one kite left lying on the ground. Maud reached to grab it when Master Graham held onto the string. "I'll do it," he said. His voice was calm, like the eye of the hurricane. He flew his kite deep into the atmosphere, along with the other eighty-four kites. "What a beautiful sight!" he said.

The sky was clear; the sun was out with a wind of fifteen miles an hour. "It feels like a normal day, beautiful and so peaceful," Maud said.

"Don't let it fool you. This is what the eye of the hurricane looks like," Paul replied.

All the kites were up in the air in twenty minutes. The buzzing sound coming from the tongue of the kites could be heard miles away. The tails of the kites were whipping to and from as the kites went higher into the sky. Everyone held on to their kites, dancing and singing, "The Kites of Love will bring us deliverance. We pray to you, O God. They chanted the chorus several more times. The wind was now thirty miles per hour, with a light sprinkle of rain. Maud gave the orders, "Let go of your kites, everyone!" Then with an enormous cry, as if talking to her parents in person, she said, "See you soon, Mama and Papa!"

Paul mumbled under his breath, "See you soon, brother."

The Kites of Love applauded as they let go of their kites and shouted again, "Deliverance, deliverance!"

The kites took off high into the atmosphere; it was a magnificent sight. As the wind speed increased, higher and higher the kites went into the heavens until they were a tiny dot then vanished forever. The wind was now about forty miles an hour. Paul shouted, "Let's go now!"

They disembarked from Deliverance. MamaJames, Nanne, and the children sat on their bottom, pulling themselves down the hill, afraid of falling. The downward grade of the hill was slippery, filled with leaves and rain deposited on the ground from the hurricane. Master Graham followed suit, as his leg was still a little sore from the fall earlier. The rain was falling harder as they made their way half down the hilly slope, slipping and sliding from the stream of flowing water. They held onto tiny plants and grass, digging their hands into the ground to break their fall. Nanne tried to stand as she reached the end of the slope. She lost their balance, tumbling over. "Oh my god," she cried.

Master Graham laughed as he collided with Nanne's head. The laughter spread to everyone. Master Graham was a part of The Kites of Love, whether he believed it or not. He was welcome. It was a significant accomplishment, a moment in history. The kites were flown, and everyone had fun, including Master Graham.

Master Graham and some of the workers hurriedly helped the children and the seniors to the harvest house as the hurricane was at their heels. Maud ran into the harvest house and took hold of her mother's pillow. She held the pillow above her head and spoke to it, as if talking to her mother, "We did it, Mama. Mama, we did it." She then put the pillow to her chest, her heart pounding as she imagined feeling her mother's heartbeat through the pillow. "I love you, Mama and Papa. See you soon." The tears flowed, warming her cold cheek. Maud broke her connection from her mother's pillow when she heard a rumbling sound: the master's voice.

"Thanks for the adventure, but everyone needs to leave when the hurricane passes," Master Graham said. He then made a U-turn and walked from the harvest house to his house.

Maud walked to where everyone gathered. She expressed frustration. "I don't understand the master's change of mood. How can he be so mean!" she said.

MamaJames consoled her granddaughter. "It will be fine. We flew our kites, didn't we?"

The eye of the hurricane passed seven minutes later. The wind speed, now 120 miles per hour, was more powerful, like a million horses galloping. The blowing debris exploded on the building like a canon. The south side window shattered, with glass and other debris flying everywhere. The children screamed.

MamaJames shouted, "Everyone, hide! Hide under the tables, and stay away from the windows."

The tables were huge, made of lignum vitae wood, tough, and strong. They were happy to have them to use as a shield, protection from flying objects coming through the window. The hurricane lasted until noon that day. The wind speed was down to seventy miles per hour now, a tropical storm. Heavy rain and flying debris could be heard outside, making it dangerous for everyone to leave. They all gathered around, telling stories of their kite-flying adventure and playing games.

Maud turned to her grandma. "What now? We flew our kites, Grandma. Do you think they will ever get to Cuba, and do you think Mama and Papa will get the kites?"

MamaJames put her hands on Maud's cheeks. With a perplexed look, she replied, "I don't know. We can only hope."

Paul was walking with his mama when he overheard Maud's conversation with her grandma. He extended his hand to Maud and his aunt, inviting them to walk with him. He clutched them under his arm. He needed that family connection and the warmth of each body bonding. He then looked down at Maud and his aunt and saw the sadness in their eyes, the loneliness and the absence of a loved one. The shadow from their eyes transformed to his with tear-filled eyes. He felt their pain. He too lost his younger brother to Cuba. He missed his younger brother so much; they were like twins.

"It is a good thing we did, flying our kites. I believe many of the kites will wash up on the shores of Cuba," Paul continued. This was a great undertaking. We will overcome and reward our loved ones."

He turned and looked in his mother's eyes, and with a fist in the air of confidence, he repeated, "We will overcome."

Maud believed in her uncle's words. It was like Scripture. The tears of sadness turned into tears of joy. Her face lit up with a big smile, putting her doubt at rest.

"Let's dance!" Paul shouted. "We have a lot to celebrate."

Everyone was on their feet as Nanne led them in songs. The men used the tables as drums, beating it to the tune of the songs, while the females clapped their hands and stamped their feet. The sound of the thunderclaps and the debris hitting on the side of the house brought some spice to their celebration. Kites of Love celebrated for hours.

The day had gone by fast. It was 4:00 p.m., and everyone was getting hungry. They had exhausted all the food they brought with them. Paul ordered everyone to return to his house. The storm was weakening with forty miles of wind speed with a light rain. They covered their heads and bodies with the huge tablecloths. They walked in groups, sheltering the children and the senior adults and making a barrier from the flying debris. Paul and his sons made dinner as the women rested. He dug up the food he buried in the ground. Everyone ate the cold food, as it was impossible to get the wood fire going to heat the food up. Paul wanted so much to please his master and do as he requested, getting everyone out of the harvest house. But his house was tiny compared to the harvest house. The odor coming from everyone was powerful, a mold-like smell from the wet clothes. The ground was wet and cold, which made it impossible to sit. They all gathered around, standing and eating their food. It was uninhabitable for everyone to stay at Paul's house.

Paul realized that he had to do something and do it fast.

"I will have to move you all back to the harvest house."

The news was a relief to all, especially to MamaJames. She shouted, "Thank God."

She knew it was a breathing ground for germs, and she would rather go back to the harvest house in the storm than stay in her nephew's house. MamaJames grabbed her herbal bag to doctor anyone who needed attention. Everyone did their part by bringing supplies with them to last until it was suitable to return. They walked back to the harvest house, sheltering with the tablecloths while protecting the seniors and the children as they walked.

Everyone changed into dry clothes. Paul, his sons, and some men built a fireplace in the harvest house. They used bricks and stones to hold the wood in place. Once the fire was lit, they brought over several aluminum zinc from the mechanical house. They scattered their clothes atop the aluminum zinc and placed them close to the fire. The heat from the fire dried their clothes fast. MamaJames took out some cerasee bush from her herbal bag and drew it into tea on the fire. She made the tea in an enormous pot then offered the tea to everyone. Cerasee tea is used in Jamaica for many ailments to purge and detox the body. MamaJames thought the cerasee would be good for all, chasing out the feverish condition caused from walking in the rain and wind and adding warmth to their bodies. The children had no choice; they hated the bitter taste, but they had to drink it for their own good. MamaJames added a lot of sugar to kill the bitter taste. The adults knew the benefits of the cerasee tea and drank it without sugar. MamaJames and Nanne didn't take any chances with just the cerasee tea for health benefits. They rubbed the children's faces and limbs with bay rum to chase out their feverish conditions from their bodies.

The scent of the cerasee, mixed with bay rum, filled the house with a more welcoming scent than the funk of wet clothes.

CHAPTER 9

Two days had passed, and the storm had traveled on. The weather was eighty-five degrees; the sun was blocked by the thick clouds, causing the day to look gray, but it was a welcoming sight to all. They were free to venture out.

MamaJames and her sister led the way back to Paul's house. They carried all their personal stuff to get ready for their journey back home. Andrew and his brother got the mule carts from the mechanical house and followed along.

Paul was pleased to see the other workers showed up for work. He now had a full staff. He led the workers through the grounds of the estate, examining the damage caused by the hurricane. He delegated each worker a task.

"Paul, Paul!" yelled the master.

Paul walked alongside his master as they talked. "I have inspected the hurricane damage to my place. It's bad." He continued, "I have a proposal. Your family could work to get

93

this place cleaned up in a couple days. In exchange for using the harvest house during the hurricane."

Paul's shoulders grew taller as he chuckled out a big laugh in sarcasm of the master's plea. "You're not serious, sir?" Paul asked. Paul couldn't believe what the master was asking.

The proposal disgusted Paul, and the frown on his face was visible to his master.

"My family is tired and ready to go home. I don't think this will be good," Paul said as he stared in the distance as his family were walking to his house. Master Graham was desperate and would not take no for an answer. He trotted toward Paul's family, shouting, "Nanne, Maud, stop please!"

Maud turned around as the voice traveled through the wind to her ears.

"It's Master Graham... Hold up, everyone!" she said.

Master Graham caught up to the group with one hand on his hip and the other on his chest as he labored to breathe. Taking several breaths through his mouth, he said, "I need some extra hands to clean up the hurricane debris. Will you work for me?" the master said.

The group looked at one another in dismay.

"Yes, we will!"

"Thank you. I will pay you all. Thanks again," Master Graham said. Not everyone agreed with Nanne's decision speaking for all. There was an uproar of conflicting opinions.

"It's the least we can do. We stayed in the harvest house during the hurricane, and the master helped us fly our kites," Nanne barked back.

The uproar subsided as Maud agreed with her aunt. MamaJames added, "God made the way. We should be grateful."

The group made a U-turn and headed back to the harvest house and unloaded their belongings. Paul wasn't happy with his mother's decision for the group to work but went along with it. He delegated tasks for everyone, children to the seniors.

Within two days, the estate grounds were cleared of hurricane debris. The Kite of Love crew picked up broken tree branches, raked grass, lay down landscape stone, and cleaned the harvest house. Paul and his fully staffed workers attended to the more strenuous tasks, replacing windows and repairing the roof.

Master Graham was ecstatically happy with the outcome. It was as if the hurricane missed his property. Master Graham paid everyone down to the children. He pulled Maud aside. "Walk with me. I know you're trying to find your parents in Cuba. That was what the kite-flying mission was for. I know some plantation owners in Cuba and will contact them to look out for the kites and search for your parents."

"Oh my god! Would you do that?" Maud asked.

"Yes, yes!" Master Graham replied.

"Thank you, sir," replied Maud.

Master Graham held out his hand. Maud grabbed hold of his hand and shook it as a gesture of respect and thanks. The handshake took longer than usual. Master covered their hands with his left hand to convey trust and loyalty. "You are a very brave girl. Thanks to you and your family, you have a job here when you get older."

"Thanks, sir," Maud said.

Maud headed back to the group, skipping with enthusiasm with every step she took. As The Kites of Love crew looked on, their stares were filled with astonishment and complexity at the action of the master. Maud realized that she had to explain the meeting. Their eyes were bulging out of their sockets. "What, what!" she asked with a big grin on her face. Maud told the good news. With claps of applause, they were all happy for her.

MamaJames gave her granddaughter an enormous hug. "I'm so proud of you. I told you to have faith. God will make a way."

MamaJames thought to herself, *My granddaughter pulled this off. She was a leader who orchestrated a group of family members and friends to make The Kites of Love possible. So blessed and intelligent. She made a great impact on the master.*

MamaJames couldn't hold back her thoughts. She shouted, "Maud, Maud, you're loved!"

* * *

The Kites of Love packed their belongings and said their goodbyes to Paul and his family. Maud thanked the workers and Uncle Paul and his family for helping.

"No, no, I need to thank you all," said Uncle Paul. "It thrilled the master, the work we did before and after the hurricane. Because of you all, I got a raise. Thanks again for everything."

Paul gave Maud a big kiss. "Come back and visit soon."

Maud had a lot to think of as she rode in the cart. So much gratitude from everyone. The gratitude humbled her, and she realized that she made a difference. But she had an excellent family—a family that believed and stood by her. She raised her hands in the air, giving God the glory. "Thank God," she rejoiced.

The ride home was less hectic. Maud was happy to be home and sleeping in her own bed with her mother's pillow. Maud talked to her pillow every night before she went to bed. Her message was the same: "I love you, Mama and Papa. Hope to see you soon." The words filled her with happy emotions. Maud fell asleep immediately every night.

CHAPTER 10

The hurricane arrived in Cuba two days later and increased to a category four with a wind speed of 150 miles per hour. The hurricane severely hit Pinar del Río and destroyed other areas of Cuba.

In its path, the hurricane destroyed Jon and Ann's house completely to the ground. The wooden shack they called home was no match for this powerful hurricane. Nothing was salvageable; they lost everything. They escaped with the clothes on their backs.

Everything they worked for went down in water and wind. Their money, the savings that they stored in tin cans, rolled away in the wind along with the flying debris. Jon and Ann were furious and ready to risk their lives to find their savings. Jon concocted a plan with his wife to find the cans of money during the eye of the hurricane. They sheltered at a nearby church to wait out the hurricane.

A calm came over the church, and for the first time, they could hear themselves talk without shouting over the flying debris hitting the sides and the roof of the church. The eye of the hurricane was here.

Jon and Ann dashed out the church doors, running down the street, jumping over debris like a track star hurdle jumper. They stirred up curiosity among the other shelterers, and they could hear footsteps running behind them. Jon took a peak over his shoulders.

"Run, Ann, run. They're on our heels!" Jon shouted.

They arrived at their homesite fifteen minutes later. They went through the debris looking for their money cans or any piece of metal that shone beneath the rubble of debris. "Over here, I found some, Ann!" Jon shouted.

There were six other people searching for their gold. They came running like their names were Ann. They jumped on Jon, knocking him to the ground, and stole his pesos like pirates. Jon and Ann fended them off, but there were too many of them. Jon threw a tree branch at them in anger. "You thieves!" he cried.

The hurricane pirates ran down the road to another shelter.

Jon and Ann continued looking. They had four more money cans and pursued desperately to find them. Ann found one money can and hid it between her breasts. Jon was not as lucky to find a money can but found some coins on the ground. The wind had picked up, blowing debris in their direction.

"It's time to go back to the church. The hurricane is coming back," Ann said.

With a big smile on their faces, they were happy. "One money can is better than none," shouted Ann as she ran. They got back in the shelter just in time as the eye of the hurricane passed.

"We have to go back out when the hurricane passes. Eight years of our life savings and all our possessions in pieces swimming away to the sea. We have to find our money. That's all we got!" Jon said.

Jon and Ann sheltered in the church for two days while the hurricane passed, and it was safe. The eye of the hurricane had blown the debris away from their house. So Jon and Ann ran in the opposite direction of their house site. They combed through the rubble for hours, along with other property owners, trying to find any valuables. Ann found a money can and picked up a handful more coins. Ann kept the treasures to herself and later met up with Jon and told him of her findings. "It's time to go. Let's go!" Ann begged, as she was tired and wet from digging through the foot and half of water.

Jon dragged his legs. He too was tired. His face showed pain of disappointment. He didn't find a money can and wasn't ready to walk away. As he swallowed his saliva, it tasted bitter—bitter of eight years of hardship. It filled his stomach and drove him with a belly ache of desire to find the last money can or the equivalent of scattered pesos. He understood his wife's pain, but the pain of losing his savings was greater. "I will stay out here a little longer. You can go!"

Jon searched for many more hours, picking up a few coins here and there. He made friends with the other property owners and helped them find their stuff. The causes were mutual; everyone was trying to find anything belonging to them. They helped one another as they displayed trust. Jon helped them and hoped to get help in return.

"Encouragement sweetens labor," he mumbled to himself. As he toiled away, he fostered a strategy to make friends then make them into an army if he ever needed them to help him fight for his wealth. Jon helped his neighbors for hours, way into the evening. He declined their gifts for help. Hungry and tired, he pushed on, winning their trust.

In the far distance, Jon saw a group of people running toward them. Jon recognized the group as the people who robbed him three days ago. Jon crouched down, hunched his shoulders forward to hide his face, waiting for them to get closer. He whispered to a couple of his neighbors, telling them of his misfortune. He felt their loyalty. Jon shouted, "Let's get them!"

They surrounded the hurricane pirates, an army of twenty neighbors. They armed themselves with tree branches and whatever debris they could find. Jon's army stood ready to defend and defeat.

Jon, like a major, stood ahead of the army in command. "Give me back my money, or we will have to defend, beat you to dirt!" Jon said. The hurricane pirates returned to Jon the can of money they stole.

Jon took his gaze away from the hurricane pirates. He looked down at the cans in his hands; he was happy. His mind was floating in the wind as the happiness he felt engulfed him. The weapon fell from his hands. He became an easy target, as if distracted from his military duties. Then a cry like from a platoon of soldiers, defeated and conquered, his neighbor cried. Jon stood up to his aggressors, the anger swelling up on his face. Jon picked up the stick with his dominant hand and gave the command, "Let's beat these pirates!"

The neighbors came through for Jon, striking the thieves vigorously and chasing them away, crying. Jon came out of the war with the thieves victoriously. He thought to himself, *You will never rob again, you bastards*.

Jon thanked his neighbors and ran back to the church to be with his wife. Jon told Ann of his adventure and of retrieving their money.

They both changed into dry clothes they got from the church. Jon and Ann stayed at the church for two more days, getting their thoughts together and hoping that the hurricane pirates would be long gone. They traveled north of the island, least hit by the hurricane, to find work and settle.

Ann hid the money in cloths, in bundles of three. She then tied it around her waist, pulling on her blouse to hide the bulge. Jon put some coins in his pocket for immediate use. They set out on their journey to Havana, stopping at different shelters for food and overnight stays. They arrived in Havana two and a half days later. They bought fares for the urban tramway train, to the farthest point north, taking them to the end of the train track, the terminal. The hurricane had devastated this province, so Jon and Ann traveled further northeast, hoping to settle where the hurricane was less severe. They mainly traveled by foot and occasionally hitched rides from mule carts driven by Negroes. They arrived in the province of Guantanamo.

Guantanamo was situated at the Caribbean Sea with Haiti to one side and Jamaica to the other side. To their surprise, there were many Black immigrants from Jamaica. They felt at home and settled. They secured a job on a small plantation and started working immediately. On the plantation, there were two groups of workers. The workers living on the plantation worked seven days a week, and the other workers who commute worked five days a week. The commuters made more wages than those living on the plantation. The difference in wages was used to board the workers who lived on the plantation.

The Jamaican workers would often say, "We like it here. We can see the backyard of our birth home." Jon and Ann made friends with their Jamaican countrymen and would listen to their weekend stories when they returned to work after their weekend days off. The workers living on the plantation were denied leaving the property unless it was a slow day. So Jon and Ann looked forward to the stories every Monday. The stories were told in Jamaican and Cuban dialect, filled with drama and suspense and at times head swelling with excitement.

This week, the stories were a little different. The storyteller revealed, "The hurricane had dumped kites on the shore." The seashore was filled with kites, the frame, paper, and kite tail.

"It's a mystery!" the storyteller said.

Jon and Ann listened, intrigued by the story. They concluded that this was a very strange story.

The days came and went. So did the stories of the kites. It became an everyday occurrence, and everyone was giving their own version. Ann inhaled the stories of the kite every day and breathed it out every night, causing sleepless nights. She mumbled to herself, "Why would anyone do this?"

* * *

It was Friday evening. The workers had left for home. Ann felt the emptiness, missing the workers and their adventurous stories. She thought, *I would love to go places and do things and not be stuck here.*

Ann told her husband that staying here was killing her. "I needed to get out," she cried. The stories of the kites were very good, but she needed to see for herself. She confided in her husband. She would claim to be sick and needed to get out to buy some bush cold medicine from the market. They concocted the story and hoped that it would work. Jon was excited for his wife but fearful that the master might not believe her or there were too many tasks to complete and wouldn't let her go.

Ann was up most of the night, thinking of the world beyond the plantation. She wanted to be a storyteller instead of a story listener.

Ann was barred from talking face-to-face with the master. The foreman was the link of communication between the workers and the master, a chain of command. Ann approached the foreman and told him that she was sick and needed to get some bush medicine at the market.

The foreman looked through his work roster. "It's a very busy day. We need all the workers here today," he replied.

Ann tried to be convincing, letting out a big cough then forcing herself to sneeze by rubbing her nose with pepper that she hid in the palm of her hand. "Am sorry!" Ann said. Rubbing her nose again, she sneezed several more times

"I will have to run this through with the master," said the foreman.

Jon was waiting in the near distance and overheard the conversation and wanted to help his wife. He held his hands in the air as a gesture to get the foreman's attention. The foreman acknowledged Jon.

"Yes, Jon!" the foreman said.

"I can work longer hours to make up for Ann's workload."

The foreman walked toward the great house, not responding to Jon's proposal.

An hour later, the foreman appeared. The decision was in his hand, told to him by his master. "I am sorry." The foreman looked dead straight in Ann's eyes. "The master said you had to work!" The foreman laid down the law.

Ann was devastated and angry. She mumbled under her breath, "You half-breed. You think you're in charge of me." She spoke poorly of the foreman. The foreman was a mulatto, half-European and half-African. His complexion was dominantly pink. He looked European, except for his woollike hair.

She pleaded with him to let her go. "You must know about these cold medicines that we used to cure the cold with. I need to go to the market to buy this bush."

Ann was implying that the foreman was Black and grew up in a similar culture as hers.

The foreman became mad at Ann's remarks. "I am in charge and certainly not a Negro like you, so get to work, you animal."

Ann felt defeated and humiliated. Her eyes swelled with tears tickling her throat. Ann crouched over, coughing many times to clear the tears from her throat and nose and throwing up mucus. Jon consoled his wife, burying her face in his shoulders. The foreman looked from a distance and saw Ann coughing up mucus. He walked over to where they were standing.

"I don't want you infecting everyone. Get off my property. Go get your damn bush. And for you, boy, Jon, I will work you to the dust you came from."

Jon was smiling not because he was going to die from overwork but because his wife was going on an adventure—an adventure that she would die for if she didn't get to go.

Ann wiped the tears from her eyes and cleared her throat. She smiled inside; she was happy.

Ann went to her sleeping quarters and took out some money for travel and food then changed into clean clothes. Once off the property, Ann skipped her way to the market; she was happy. She greeted everyone on the road with a broad smile. Ann bought her cerasee bush at the market. She needed to prove that she was ill. Then she bought food for her adventure. Ann walked around, taking in everything the small town had to offer. Free like a bird, she could fly to wherever she desired.

Ann met up with one of her coworkers. They were having so much fun; she smiled and said, "Anywhere is better than working where you live. Let's go to the beach. You know where the kites were found."

They arrived at the coast forty minutes later. The sea banks were practically bare; the debris was gone. Ann walked along the shore, looking for anything to be a good story-teller. Ann saw some kite frames sticking out of the sea sand. She bent down to pick up the kite frame when pieces of kite paper attached to the frame uprooted; she examined the paper but could not read the writing; it was too water soaked from being buried in the wet sand.

Ann and her coworker looked around like journalists, trying to find anything to compose a wonderful story. There were kite tails and more kite papers in a pile by an almond tree trunk five hundred yards from the shore. Ann smiled when she saw the debris; it was gold to her eyes. She rummaged through the kite's remains. There was writing on the tail and on the tongue of the kites. The kite paper resembled handwriting paper and the text faded beyond recognition. Ann became more intrigued. She wondered to herself, *What is this? Who could have done this?*

She put the paper and tail from the kite in her food bag. She had proof to show to her husband. Ann enjoyed her time at the sea and the treasures she found. She thanked her friend for his company and her adventure.

"I only have one regret," she said to the friend. "I would love to have been here a week ago to see the kites scattered over the shore. I love to read what they wrote on the kites before nature destroyed them."

Her head was full as she tried to process the kite's remains. "Maybe it's a puzzle for someone to solve, or it could be a message sent by a loved one. People have been sending messages and messengers for years, like in the Bible when Noah sent the bird out of the ark when the flood ended. But a message in the form of kites, that is great," she concluded with an intriguing grin.

CHAPTER 11

"My younger brother picked up some of the kites a day after they were washed up on the shore. He reads English and Spanish very well. He brought them home to dry so he could read them later," said the coworker.

"Can I see your brother now?" Ann asked.

"He lives in another town. Maybe another day or when he is done reading, I can ask him to let you have them," the coworker said.

"That would be great!" replied Ann.

Ann arrived at the plantation an hour later. The foreman searched her bags, looking for the cold bush. "You are late. Where have you been?"

"I went to the sea to take a dip. The salt water is good when you're sick," Ann replied.

"Well, cook your cold tea, rest for one hour, then go back to work. If you have so much faith in this bush, you should be ready to work in an hour. Do I make myself clear?" said the foreman.

"Yes, sir," replied Ann.

Ann drew her cerasee tea, drank two cups, then laid her treasures at the head of the mattress. She lay on her mattress, looking up at the ceiling. Her body was resting, but her brain was on fire, intrigued with finding the kite's remains. She couldn't get her brain to cool down. Her thoughts flowed. *I wish I could see Jon to tell him of my adventure and stories.*

With a big smile, she shouted, "I am now a storyteller."

The hour went by fast. Ann worked past everyone, making up for the time she was gone. After dinner, she thought she was done working but was wheeled out by the foreman in the field with her lantern to work. Jon was also pulled from his mattress to work in the field alongside his wife.

"There you go. You said you would work double for your wife," the foreman shouted at Jon.

Ann was happy to see her husband and work with him. It was hard to have a conversation as the foreman was watching. She so desperately wanted to tell her story. After four hours, they were finished working and were set free to go to bed.

Ann sat outside their sleeping quarters with her husband. The crickets chirped, breaking the silence as the heavens lit up the atmosphere with an array of stars, a perfect scenery for telling her story. Ann began talking, her body giving off different gestures as her voice caressed her words to amplify her story. The kite story was long but very interesting as Jon's stare was fixed on his wife's face.

"I felt like I was there. Such a very beautiful story," remarked Jon.

Ann was happy with her husband's praises and felt proud of being a storyteller.

Ann was up early the next morning. She checked the kite scraps, her treasures, if they were dry to read. As she checked, she set aside the dry paper in a pile. Then she joined the pieces of paper together like a puzzle. She was trying to make sense of the words or symbols. The markings on the paper faded from the hurricane and were hard to decipher. Ann didn't give up. Like a detective, she worked tirelessly.

"Ann, Ann, it's time for work," Jon called out.

"Do I have to?" Smiling as she put the kite scraps away, she continued, "It's like trying to solve a puzzle with missing pieces."

It was Monday. The workers each revealed their stories of their different adventures. Ann listened but found it boring. She had her own story in a bundle of kite scraps and couldn't wait for work to end to go back to her puzzle. Ann worked on solving her kite scraps until it was too dark to see.

She resumed as soon as she woke up. "Ha!" Ann screamed in excitement. "I found a piece of paper with 'Ma'!"

Ann was the first one out the door for work. She was filled with excitement, which showed in her work performance.

The foreman commented, "Good job, Ann!"

Ann continued working on the kite scraps every morning and night. She found a few more letters but couldn't make a word.

* * *

The week was coming to an end. It was Friday morning. The coworker that met Ann at the sea had some news from his brother.

"My brother found the name 'Maud' and…and some other words," said the coworker.

Ann shouted, "Maud! Who is Maud?"

"My brother said to look at the kite tails. There is also writing on the tail of the kites," the coworker added.

Ann replied, "Thanks, I will." Ann thought to herself, *The only Maud I know is my daughter in Jamaica. No, no*! She dismissed this thought from her mind. *It's probably a spelling error. I too have found "Ma"… Letters, but no words.*

Ann needed to see for herself and wanted to meet the coworker's brother. She couldn't claim sickness again. It was the weekend, and she would not see her coworker until Monday. The intrigue was driving her crazy. She prayed for a miracle. She thought that the church would give her that miracle. Ann remembered working at other plantations; the masters allowed churchgoing. Ann talked to the foreman for the workers to go to church. This was one privilege the workers had: leaving the plantation to attend church. Ann stood ahead of the workers and went to battle for this cause. The foreman gathered that Ann was a troublemaker. He mumbled under his breath, "This Negro is always trying to make the rules and will do anything to get out of work." He also knew she wasn't a fool. She was right; this was a privilege.

The master encouraged churchgoing for the workers, and the foremen had to honor this request.

The workload for the weekend was very heavy, but the foreman had to honor this privilege.

The foreman announced churchgoing for everyone on Sundays for four hours and four hours of work upon their return.

Ann screamed in excitement; her voice was louder than the other workers'.

Her voice traveled deep into the banana field. This was a cry of freedom. "Oh my god!" she cried.

The workers ran down the rows of the banana plants with big smiles, skipping and dancing. It was a victory.

The birds flew over their heads as if celebrating with them; they were free—free like the birds.

After their victory laps, Ann shouted, "The foreman was good to us. Let's work with all our might. Let's make him proud."

After such a breakthrough, Ann appointed herself the leader of the workers, subforeman, jokingly she named herself.

"You earned it, standing up for us all," Jon said to his wife. He was so proud, with a big smile on his face. The workers pressed on working, boosted with strength of happiness, working through their lunch break.

Everyone was up early on Sunday morning. They left at dawn so they could have a longer time to themselves, adding two more extra hours to their time off. As they exited the plantation, the sound of singing and stamping of feet could be heard in the wind.

"Thanks, Ann!" the workers shouted.

"Remember to be back by noon," Ann replied.

Ann and Jon walked down to the sea, where she found the kites. They were sitting on the seashore as they looked in the directions of Haiti then Jamaica. Jon tried to solve the mystery of the kites.

"If the kites were found here, then they came from the north, which points toward Jamaica," Jon said.

"You're right!" said Ann.

"But who could have sent them, and why?" she added.

The thoughts lingered in their mind as they walked to church. The church ceremony was very inspiring, with many hidden messages. The pastor preached about family.

The pastor quoted from the Bible, "As a bird that wandereth from her nest, so is a man that wandereth from his place [Proverbs 27:8 KJV]."

The preacher continued, "Families leave their children for greener pastures, leaving the burden for someone else to take their role."

The preacher gave another illustration of a family who abandoned their family: "When my father and my mother forsake me, then the Lord will take me up [Psalm 27:10 KJV]."

The pastor preached to the congregation, but it was like he was talking to Ann and Jon.

Ann asked for a miracle, and she received one. God was speaking to her through the pastor. She didn't realize this even though she replied "Amen" many times during the ceremony, giving her confirmatory response.

Ann and Jon met up with the coworker. They walked to his brother's house so Ann could look at the pieces of the kite scraps.

Ricardo walked through the wooden door of his house, holding the kite scraps, his scrawny figure struggling to contain them in his arms. Ann and Jon introduced themselves to Ricardo.

Ricardo took two steps backward. His eyes lit up as his brow creased on his forehead. He looked like he saw a ghost. "What's wrong?" Ann said.

"Look for yourself," Ricardo said.

Ann looked over his shoulders at the faded prints and the torn papers where he pasted together to make words. The words spelled out "Ann" and "Jon."

Ricardo continued, "And I suppose these people are your family, Maud and MamaJames?"

Ann fell to the ground. Her knees hit the earth hard, the crackling sound resembling broken bones. Ann was speechless as the tears run down her cheeks and made an enormous mud splash on the ground. The ground was also filled with blood from the contact with her knees, but the revelation cut her heart in a million pieces.

Her cry, like a thousand voices, was traveling in the wind. Jon knelt down next to his wife, unable to hold back his manly emotions. The mud splash grew bigger with his tears.

The church bell rang for the 10:00 a.m. church service.

*　*　*

Jon and Ann were still at Ricardo's house and would be late returning to work if they didn't leave now.

Ann took the kite's tail from Ricardo and looked at the writings for similarities. Though faded, she could read the names and words: "Ann," "Jon," and "love, Maud and Mama."

Her emotion peaked to madness, filled with grief and despair rolling on the ground. She tore her clothes from her body like Reuben in the Bible when he betrayed his younger brother Joseph. Ann was acting out in the same manner. She had betrayed her mother and daughter.

Jon slapped his wife continuously on her cheeks, as if waking her up from an insane nightmare.

"Stop, Ann, stop!" Jon called out to his wife.

Ann sat up and composed herself. She lost all the buttons from her blouse, exposing her breast, when she tore her clothes off. Ann tied both ends of her blouse together to keep it in place covering her breast. Her white clothes were different shades of brown and filled with dirt from rolling around on the ground. Her face had three tones of color from crying as the earth stuck to her face like a warrior's mask. "You're dirty," said Jon.

"I have to go back to Jamaica to be with my little girl and Mama," Ann said as she wiped the tears from her eyes with the back of her hands. The news was devastating; it destroyed them.

Ricardo solved the mystery, bringing words to life.

"Am indebted to you. Thanks, Ricardo," Ann said.

Ann and Jon held hands, walking back to the plantation. They were two hours late and fifty minutes away.

"We have to go back home. This is phenomenal, flying kites to get to us. Oh my god!" Ann repeated herself.

"We have to go back to Jamaica," Ann rattled on, nervous and worried as the tears washed the dirt off her face. "The pastor was talking to us. The message in his ceremony, the message of family."

Ann recited one verse the pastor quoted: "'When my father and mother forsake me the Lord will take me up.' The Lord took care of Maud and somehow brought her to us as kites. She must have something to do with the kites reaching the shores of Cuba."

Jon agreed with his wife and the revelation of Ricardo.

"The church ceremony was definitely meant for us," he said, drawing his words, as if clinging to every word as it came from his mouth and realizing that everything that happened was true.

"It's a miracle. I asked for a miracle, and I received one. Praise the Lord," Ann said.

Jon listened to his wife, agreeing with everything she said. He kept his emotions locked away inside of him, but he was hurting as much as she was. He had to stay strong for her.

"Why aren't you saying anything!" Ann cried. "It's been eight years, eight years since we left Jamaica. We are going back. We have to."

"I totally agree," Jon said.

The foreman was waiting for Jon and Ann; they defied his orders. "You are late! I hope you have a good explanation for walking in here so late!" the foreman yelled.

Jon grabbed hold of his wife's hand, and as their eyes met, the truth had to come out. No more lying to themselves or to others.

Jon related the story of the kites to the foreman.

"That's impossible!" he continued. "I wonder what will happen next week. A man will go to the moon." The foreman smiled sarcastically. "You are fired! This is not a fairyland."

The foreman walked to the great house.

The master came out; they talked for a while.

With the revelation of the kites and now being fired, Ann said, "A day of reckoning and reflection of greatness and sadness."

The foreman approached Jon and Ann. "The master, Mr. Gomez, would like to see you both."

CHAPTER 12

No one had ever been called to the great house or talked with the master. All communication went through the foreman. Jon and Ann were bewildered by the master's request. So was the foreman. It puzzled him.

Jon and Ann hurried with long strides, their heads facing the ground, avoiding eye contact with the master. They knew their place.

Mr. Gomez was standing on the veranda of his house. The puffs from his cigar filled the veranda, casting a colossal figure to his already overweight body. "Would you like to talk in English or Spanish?"

"English, sir," Jon replied.

The master was of European descent. He spoke in a deep husky voice, coughing occasionally from the smoke of the cigar deposited in his throat. "The foreman told me he fired you because of some crazy story you made up. That story is actual. I traveled to the ocean to see the remains of the hurricane damage. That's when I saw kite scraps on the shore of the ocean."

The master excused himself, placed his half-smoked cigar in a large wooden bowl, and walked into his house. Jon and Ann were astonished and yet thrilled that the master believed them.

He returned a couple minutes later holding a kite, with the kite paper and tail still intact to the kite. The kite had some water damage but was in pretty good condition. He handed the kite to Jon and Ann. Ann read the words written on the kite aloud: "I love you, Mama and Papa" "Ann, Jon," and "Maud and MamaJames. See you soon." The words on the kite were legible, making it easy for Ann to read.

Jon and Ann sandwiched the kite between them, holding each other in a tight embrace. Their tears flowed, falling onto the kite. Ann let go of the embrace as her body became weak, drained from losing so much tears and the massive headache building up in her head.

She fell to the ground. The tiny pebbles on the surface of the ground pierced through Ann's sore knee, spurting blood everywhere. The master saw the anguish on Ann's face and the pain she felt, both physically and emotionally. He stepped down the veranda and stood by Jon and Ann. As he spoke, Jon and Ann sat on the ground with their heads held high. The master showed empathy, and they wanted to thank him with their eyes and heads held high. The master took a couple of puffs from his cigar then let out a big cough, clearing his lungs. Then he continued talking, "When I saw the kites on the ocean and read what was written on them, my thoughts were 'This is magnificent. A noble gesture: communication through kites.' I kept the kites, hoping someday to give it to the rightful owners.

"Greatness should not pass without rewards, so I wanted to help, not knowing that the two people on the kite were working for me. So when Mr. Graham wrote to me and asked to look out for the kites and get in touch with you and Samuel, I was happy to assist."

He continued, "I have already located your cousin at Mr. Graham's request. Mr. Graham owns the plantation in Montego, Jamaica, where your other cousin Paul works. Paul is the foreman on his plantation, a very loyal servant to Mr. Graham. Because of this loyalty, Mr. Graham would like to help his family by getting you back to Jamaica. He asked me to locate you and help you go back to Jamaica."

Jon and Ann stared up at the master rubbing their ears to make sure that they heard correctly what the master was saying. The master continued, "There is a cargo ship docked at the harbor going back to Jamaica in a week. You will travel on this ship back to Jamaica."

The master reinstated their employment. "I do not fire you. You will work the week, with one day off to gather your belongings for the ship ride home."

Ann and Jon were speechless. Their mouths dropped to the ground in astonishment. They took their eyes to heaven, thanking God. "Thank you, sir. *Muchas gracias.*" They repeated these words several more times as they trotted backward for a show of respect.

Ann and Jon hugged as they looked up in the heavens again, giving God the glory.

The foreman wasn't happy with the outcome but had to honor the master's request. His approach was very soft and respectful toward Jon and Ann. "You take the day off, and I'll see you in the morning for work," he said.

Ann and Jon walked to their sleeping quarters. They talked about everything: the kites and its revelation, master's gratitude, and going home to be with their family.

This was a miracle. They gave thanks. Ann led the prayer. Ann and Jon held hands and knelt down to pray. The words flew out of her mouth: "God and heavenly Father, we thank you for small mercy and big miracles. We have set out on this course for eight years, battered and beaten with life challenges for the sake of money. We have tried many times to get back to Jamaica. The ships were food cargo, and they denied all humans. God, thank you for the small mercies. Thank you for the hurricane. It was a blessing bringing our family closer together. Kites from our family washing up on the shores of Cuba is a miracle. Master Graham and our Master Gomez getting together for our return to Jamaica is another miracle. Thank God. *Muchas gracias*, God. Amen," Ann and Jon said.

Ann and Jon went down to the river, bathed the grief off their bodies, and washed their clothes. They felt clean and reborn in Christ's grace.

On the most famous day of the week, Monday, the stories flowed from the mouth of the workers, filled with suspense and drama. Some stories were delightful, and others were sad. The workers gravitated to each story; the connection brought them closer and improved their work performance. It was Ann's and Jon's turn to tell their stories; Ann was delightful. Her face lit up with a pleasant smile. As she opened her mouth, her body movements expressed every word. She told of the kite's story and its revelation and the master helping them go back to Jamaica. This was the best story they had ever heard. "It was a beautiful and a great ending," said the workers.

Ann was very proud to be a storyteller and was happy with her presentation as she invaded their bodies and resonated with her coworkers. She knew they were all kept captives. As the story ended, there were releases of sighs, then an enormous smile, as if they were free.

Some Jamaican working on the plantation voiced their concerns: the desire to return to their homeland, Jamaica.

Ann replied, "Don't give up. God will make a way."

* * *

The week went by like a fast breeze, and suddenly it was the day before their departure to Jamaica.

Pesos were not the currency used in Jamaica. Ann and Jon had to convert their savings to a mutual product—a product that could be beneficial in Jamaica to bring back their money plus a profit. Ann suggested to her husband to use all their savings to buy rolls of fabric so they could sell them in Jamaica to make a living. Jon agreed.

The town square was a couple of miles from the plantation. Ann put a skip in her steps.

"You are happy, honey," Jon said to his wife.

"We are going home, aren't we!" Ann replied.

They held hands. Jon showed his appreciation to his wife, giving her a kiss on her cheek. They bought some souvenirs and clothes for Maud and MamaJames and spent the rest of the money on fabric.

Jon and Ann said their goodbyes to their coworkers and the foreman.

Master Gomez used his two horse-pulled carts to transport them to the shipping dock. Jon and Ann stepped inside the cart.

This was an enclosed cart with two windows on either side of it. It had three sets of seats, two facing the front of the cart and the third facing the back of the cart. Its interior was gray with a silky textured fabric.

It was a sophisticated cart. Jon and Ann felt privileged.

Master Gomez sat on one set of seats facing the front of the cart, opposite seat to Jon and Ann. They drove to the ship in silence. Jon held hands with his wife as their fingers caressed, communicating in a speechless bond.

Paul's brother, Samuel, was on the dock waiting. They had not seen each other for almost ten years.

Ann ran to Samuel and gave him a kiss on his cheek. "I haven't seen you in ages. How are you?" Ann asked.

"I know, it's been awhile. I have been stuck here for ten years. I signed up for two years, and they refused to take us back." With tearful eyes, he continued, "I miss my family."

"Thank you. *Gracias*, Master Gomez," Ann said.

"Yes! *Gracias*, Master," Jon and Samuel said simultaneously.

"It was a pleasure," replied Master Gomez.

They shook the master's hand and boarded the ship.

The ship stewardess led them to the lower deck of the ship, where produce was stored for export.

The temperature in the lower deck was cold to keep the produce fresh but too cold for humans. They snuggled up together, using the fabric Ann bought to keep them warm. "It felt like the bonding of the prodigal children," Ann said as they reconnected with family values and their new life ahead with their families.

It would take six hours for the ship to arrive in Jamaica. The ship sounded its horn, the signal for leaving port. The horn sounded, and they knew that they were on their way home. With smiles, their hearts were full. "Thank god!" Ann shouted

The lower deck became colder as the ship sailed deeper into the high sea. It was an unbearable condition. Their bodies were freezing. They had to find ways to stay warm. They stocked some of the produce boxes around themselves and covered it with more fabric.

Their bodies became warmer, and the thought of going home filled them with a warmth of gratitude, and the freezing in their body was no more.

The ship sounded the horn six hours later. It docked. They gathered their belongings and disembarked from the ship. They kissed the ground then looked up to the heavens. "Thank you, God!" echoed from their mouths. They walked a mile from where the ship docked, greeting everyone with a fulfilling smile on their faces. It's been over eight years for Jon and Ann. They couldn't recognize anything.

"Do you know where we are?" Ann asked a fisherman.

The fisherman replied, "*Je ne comprends pas!*" It sounded like "*No comprendes*" in Spanish. They thought that they were in Jamaica and the fisherman was bilingual. Ann spoke in Spanish, hoping to get some clarity of her question.

The fisherman replied, "Haiti!"

"Haiti! We are in Haiti," they shouted. They hurried back to the dock to get back on the ship. The last of the livestock was boarding onto the ship, and the first horn sounded. The ship was leaving soon. Afraid to get stuck in another country, they ran as fast as they could with their belongings tied to their backs. They arrived at the dock and threw themselves on the boardwalk of the ship and crawled on their hands and knees up to the entrance of the ship. The ship steward held his hand in the air. "Stop! Where do you think you're going?" the steward yelled.

"We are getting back on the ship," Jon said.

"No, you're not. This is not a human cargo ship. No stowaway allowed."

"Oh my god!" Ann cried. "We were on the ship before, going to Jamaica." She continued to explain herself, "We thought we were in Jamaica. That's why we got off."

The ship sounded its horn again. Their hearts were racing, their faces were filled with fear, and they were sweating profusely. Samuel acted on his fear by running past the ship worker, then Jon pushed the ship worker to the side. They all ran into the ship, with the ship steward running behind. "Stop, you stowaways!" the steward cried.

Jon ran to the upper deck to the captain. The captain recognized them; he pulled from his pocket the note from Master Gomez. He read their names: "Jon, Samuel, and Ann."

"Yes, sir, we are!" they shouted one at a time after they heard their names.

"Go down to the lower deck, and cause no more raucous. We should be in Jamaica in eight hours."

"Thanks, sir!" they said.

They were wiping the sweat off their foreheads. "Wow! That was frightening," said Ann.

They arrived in Jamaica eight hours later. The captain announced. "We will dock in Jamaica!" The horn sounded, and the ship stopped moving. They disembarked from the ship. Once on the ground, they each knelt on both knees, kissing the ground several times, then they looked up to the heavens, with a cry to God, "Thank you, God. Thank you, God."

Samuel spotted his brother Paul at the ship dock. He dropped his bag and ran, shouting, "Paul, Paul!"

Paul turned to the sound of his name. He ran toward his brother. They hugged, locked in each other's arms. The tears from their faces were now one.

Ann and Jon walked over. Paul hugged his cousins. The tears streamed down their faces—tears of joy—as they all embraced.

It was 7:00 p.m., an hour by mule cart ride back to Paul's house. Samuel sat up in the driver's seat with his brother. The brothers talked, catching up on lost times. Ann and Jon had their own conversations. As they looked around, taking in beautiful plains and valleys, while holding hands, Jon turned to his wife. "I miss this place. I'm happy to be home."

"Me too," Ann replied with an enormous grin on her face.

Paul returned the mule cart to the mechanical house, then he walked over to the great house. Paul informed Master Graham that they had arrived.

"Good news!" replied Master Graham. "Now we have to get everyone back here for a celebration. You got work to do."

"Thanks, sir. Thank you very much for all that you have done," Paul said.

CHAPTER 13

Paul ran back to his house to be with his brother and give them the good news. It was the first week of November. Sending mail to The Kites of Love and a reply would be near Christmas.

"A Christmas celebration, great," said Paul.

"A celebration. We wanted to see Maud and Mother sooner," Ann said.

"Master Graham would like this celebration, and I think it is a great idea. Everyone should be here at the same time. The Kites of Love will celebrate your homecoming," Paul said.

He explained to Ann that there were over forty people who participated in the kite flying. "The Kites of love is what we call ourselves," Paul said.

Paul walked over to Ann and Jon. "You'll be proud of your daughter for inventing The Kites of Love," he added.

"What's that?" Ann asked.

"You'll be here for a month or longer. I will tell you all about it. We will camp at the fire every night telling stories," Paul said.

"I like stories," said Ann.

Paul was indebted to his master for bringing his family home. He put his brother, Jon, and Ann to work on the plantation. "One hand washes the other," he murmured.

Paul received a reply of his request from his relatives, The Kites of Love crew, to come to the Spice Estate to work for Christmas money. He lied. He didn't want to reveal the celebration of his brother and cousins returning home from Cuba. He felt everyone loved money and always needed more, especially on Christmastime.

Ann and Jon had settled in. They were used to hard work and fit right in with the others.

They were longing to see their daughter. The stories Paul and some workers told about Maud and her accomplishment made their hearts ache to see her more.

* * *

It had been over two months since The Kites of Love flew their kites. Maud was hoping to have some news of her parents from Master Graham.

School ended for the Christmas break. Maud and her Grandma traveled to Saint Ann for a long weekend to spend time with their relatives.

Nanne gave MamaJames the letter she received from her son Paul and asked Maud to read to her grandma. With shaking hands, Maud took the letter nervously as she unfolded the paper. She thought to herself, *Is this news about my parents?*

Maud read the letter to her grandma. As she read the complete text, it disappointed her; it wasn't what she expected. She stormed out the room, her heart full to the brim with the weight of carrying her parents.

MamaJames held her granddaughter's hand in hers. "I love you," she said, letting her know that even though she didn't get the letter she hoped for, she was loved. "You have done a lot. Give it time. I believe in you and more in God. We will prevail," said MamaJames.

Maud's emotions flipped. The sadness on her face turned to happiness as she smiled, showing off her dimples.

"Can we go, Grandma?" Maud said as her dimples got deeper. "It would be good to have extra money for Christmas."

"You may go with your aunt and cousins, but I won't be going," MamaJames said.

MamaJames, having some health issues, declined taking another trip. Her leg had gotten worse, and with fading eyesight, she didn't want to take the trip.

MamaJames discussed her state of health with her sister. They also felt that she should decline going.

"We need an iron horse to fly us there," Nanne said jokingly.

Maud told Andrew of the plans to go to the Spice Estate to work and asked if the mule carts could transport everyone.

Andrew was excited. His eyes lit up. "Work, money, yes, we will be ready," he said.

It took them a week to inform everyone of the trip.

The Kites of Love packed their stuff in the mule carts. Maud packed up her pillow atop her belongings to sit on during her journey. MamaJames traveled with the group to Saint Ann because she didn't want to stay alone. She stayed with her niece, Nanne's daughter, at their house.

It was the second week in December; the weather was cool. The tree branches swayed in the light wind, making travel a breeze. Less stopping made faster arrival.

The Kites of Love stopped in Trelawny to pick up Nanne's daughter and her family, adding to The Kites of Love group. They all bathed in the river, a custom for all who visited. The water was cool but therapeutic, as it soothed their tired muscles and cleansed their bodies. The Kites of Love set out early to Montego.

* * *

Paul set out his sons at strategic points along the route to his home to alert him when The Kites of Love was near. Paul didn't know when his family would arrive and when to have the celebration. He put his plans in gear, getting everything ready for a huge celebration. He housed his brother and cousins in his older son's home, which would be off limits to others. Paul bought food and drinks and a goat for the celebration. They decorated the harvest house with palm trees and fresh flowers picked daily and fixed these on each table. Wood stumps were placed under the tables to make up for insufficient seating.

The footsteps and the hooves of the mules could be heard a quarter mile away.

"Papa, Papa, they are coming!" shouted his son.

The brothers placed themselves a mile from the house and half a mile between one another. Paul put several pots on the wood fire to cook the celebration dinner: curried goat meat, green banana, yellow yam, white rice, and breadfruit.

The smoke from the wood fire traveled into the house through the air holes. The house had several air holes to bring in fresh air and sunlight. Ann saw the Tyndall effect as the sunlight entered the room through the tiny holes in the wall. It scattered a hazy beam of light, colliding on the opposite wall.

"Oh my god, this is beautiful. Look, look, everyone!" Ann shouted.

Ann walked to one hole with her face pressed against the wooden side of the house. She closed one eye, looking through the hole at the wood fire. There were several pots on the wood fire stove. Ann could tell the family was near. This was the sign.

"They are here," said Ann. They each took their place in the house, secured and away from the windows. As they sat still in the house, they could hear the commotion of hooves, feet, and loud chatter. They stared at one another with wide eyes and open mouths, trying to stay quiet.

Everyone got off the carts, dragging their belongings with them. Paul hugged his mama.

"Hi, Mama, you made it," he said, kissing her on the cheek. "It's good to see you."

Samuel jumped from his side of the room. He heard his mom talking. He ran to the door when Jon and Ann got hold of his arm, pulling him back to his place. "Are you crazy!" cried Jon.

It was hard for them to keep their place in the room.

Paul greeted Maud. Ann, like a bullet from a gun, ran to the door. Jon stuck out his foot, knocking her to the ground and stopping her in her tracks.

"I am going crazy here. Can I at least look through the air hole!" Ann begged.

"All right, just one of us at a time, and be careful. We don't want to spoil the surprise," said Jon.

Ann looked through the air hole, looking for her daughter and her mama, trying to picture in her mind what Maud would look like after eight years. Maud was now eleven years old. The tears bottling up in her eyes, she could not recognize her own daughter. The tears flowing from her eyes bubbled the air hole shut. Ann retreated to her place in the house as her tears rushed down her cheeks like the Dunn's River Falls. Jon consoled his wife to quiet her bawling.

Samuel looked through the air hole. Recognizing his mother, he kept his calm. He resisted with a heavy heart and restrained himself from spoiling the surprise.

Paul left his sons in charge of the cooking and led The Kites of Love group to the harvest house.

Like a wedding celebration, everyone was seated strategically in relation to their family. He then told everyone that Master Graham will be here soon to talk with them about their tasks.

The food was finished cooking and brought to the harvest house. The steam from the spicy hot food filled the house. The tantalizing aroma of the steaming curried goat sat over Maud's head. "That curried goat smells so good," said Maud.

She sat with the group as they talked about what their tasks might be. Her empty stomach roared. She was hungry, which made it harder for her to sit around waiting for the meal to be served. She walked to the door to escape. Paul blocked Maud from going through the doors.

"No one may leave. Wait patiently, Maud! You will love your task." Paul smiled.

Then the sound of cowbells were ringing for order, as if in a courthouse. Master Graham walked in, along with his wife and two children. It was the first time for his family visiting the harvest house. Master Graham invited his family to share in history and the celebration of the family returning from Cuba.

Maud murmured under her breath, "I wonder what kind of task this will be. He brought his entire family."

Master Graham stood in front of everyone, so proud of his accomplishment: uniting the family together and playing a vital role in The Kites of Love. He stood with grace and put on a smile that would hypnotize anyone.

The Kites of Love set their stare on Master Graham with their backs to the entrance of the house. So captivated, they didn't hear other footsteps entering the room.

Ann, Jon, and Samuel quietly walked into the harvest house, sat to the back behind everyone, without being recognized. The Kites of Love, hypnotized, were held in a trance by Master Graham.

He addressed The Kites of Love group. As he talked, he gestured with his hands, leaning his body into the flow of his hand gestures. And like the parting of the Red Sea, The Kites of Love verged to the left and right of the room, allowing Ann, Jon, and Samuel to walk down the aisle. And with a high pitch tone like a commentator, he announced their names as they walked to the front.

It filled Paul with chill—a chill that covered his body. It was an enormous presentation, a moment in history.

The house was filled with screams of joy, laughter, and cries. The sound bounced off the aluminum roof, echoing through the town miles away. Maud rolled on to the floor uncontrollably in a fit-like motion. Tears dribbled off her face, leaving behind puddles on the dirt floor. She cried,

"Mama, Mama, Mama and Papa, you're home! Oh my god. Thank you, God!"

Ann and Jon looked at their child rolling on the floor, crying uncontrollably. They shouted simultaneously, "That's Maud, our daughter!"

They ran to the child. "Maud, Maud, it's Mama and Papa!" they cried. They picked up Maud off the floor to their arms and hugged her. Ann pulled Maud to herself, hugging and kissing her and squeezing her into her body.

Maud's body became limp and lifeless, paralyzed from the shock of seeing her parents in front of her. Maud lay lifeless. The only movements were the tears from her eyes and sniffing sound from her nose; she was like an injured animal. The shock was too much for her.

"Maud, Maud!" Ann cried, trying to get some response, any response. Ann ran around the house for help. "Please, a mug of water."

Ann fed her daughter a sip of water from her fingertips first to her lips then into her mouth. And with a gulp then a big gasp, Maud breathed in and out, and the words flowed from her mouth. "Oh Mama, Mama, it's you. You are here. Oh my god! Oh Mama, I miss you so much. I am happy you're here," Maud cried.

"Breathe slowly," Ann tried to console her daughter.

Maud did as her mama advised until she was calm.

"I love you so, so much," said Ann.

"Me too," said Maud.

Maud walked over to her father. "Papa, I love you. I am so happy you are home," she said.

Jon gave his daughter a big hug and kiss. "You are the reason we kept going. I love you, my dear daughter," Jon said as his voice thinned out from the tears in his throat.

Maud held onto her father's hand as she skipped, walking to where her mom was waiting for them.

Samuel walked over to his mother. "Mama!" Samuel said. They held each other as tears of joy washed their faces.

"Samuel! Oh my god, you're here. I miss you so much, son! I love you. I'm happy to have you home," Nanne said.

Samuel demonstrated the prodigal son analogy. The younger son left home. His loving mother missed him more than her other son and appeared to favor him more. Samuel had migrated to Cuba to work on the plantation. He did not tell his mama or his brother he was going. Paul found out later after receiving a letter from his brother. He was disappointed in his brother for leaving and knew it would destroy their mother. Paul lied to his mother, keeping it a secret for many years. He later came to terms with his brother's decision. Paul had given up hope of ever seeing his baby brother again.

Then hope came into their lives: the possibility of contacting his brother through kite flying—an impossible task made possible when the kites were washed up on the shores of Cuba. Paul, Samuel, and their mother embraced and promised to be truthful.

The Kites of Love each greeted Jon, Ann, and Samuel, one at a time, welcoming them home.

Jon pulled his daughter between him and Ann and hugged her. With Samuel to his right side, he spoke for them. "We're very grateful to you all. Thank you!" Then he looked up, as if the ceiling wasn't there and he could see God. With a high-pitched tone, he shouted, "God, thank you! Without you, this miracle wouldn't be possible."

Then they held hands, swinging them into the air and gave God the glory.

"Attention, everyone! I have one more announcement." Master Graham stood for the second time in front of the group. "All the Jamaican immigrants in Cuba who want to come home will be able to. In collaboration with the members of parliament and the plantation owners in both countries, a movement was created. The movement for migration of immigrants will be called 'Maud,'" Master Graham said.

The harvest house was filled with screams, like it was on fire, with dancing and shouting of enjoyment.

Master Graham congratulated Maud. "You're a brave young lady. Be proud of your achievements."

"Thank you very much, Master Graham," Maud replied.

"Well, you all enjoy yourselves and have a splendid night. You have a lot to celebrate," Master Graham said.

Master Graham and his family shook hands and gave hugs to everyone as they exited the harvest house.

"Where is Mama?" asked Ann.

"Grandma has been sickly lately, and her eyesight and leg had gotten worse. She didn't want to take the trip, so she is staying with her niece at grandaunt's house," Maud said.

"Well, when she sees me, she will feel better," said Ann.

"She sure will," replied Maud.

The signature food for all celebrations and dances were served: curried goat meat and rice; yellow yam and green bananas; roasted breadfruit and callaloo. It was a feast—a celebration feast. The grand meal was well received. The dinner plates were cleaned down to the last rice grain.

The celebration lasted way into the wee hours of the morning, with dancing, singing, and small and large group chattering.

Maud approached her uncle Paul. As she walked toward him, her smile got bigger. "So, Uncle, did we really come here to work?" Maud asked.

"No!" He shared her smile. "No! You were tricked in coming. We had to get you here for the celebration. Now, isn't that a big payday?" Paul concluded.

"Yes! Yes, yes, thanks, Uncle Paul."

"Okay, hero," said Paul.

"What?" she replied.

Paul held onto Maud's hand as she turned to walk away.

"This is big stuff. You're famous, a hero. The movement of Black immigrants from Cuba back to Jamaica will be named after you." He smiled as he patted her on the shoulder. With a sarcastic smile, he said, "You'll be in history books."

They both laughed uncontrollably. Maud held onto her stomach. "It hurts from laughing so hard." She caught her breath and said in a giggly voice, "That's a pillow of love."

"I'm proud of you, cousin," Paul said.

CHAPTER 14

Maud walked over to where her belongings were and picked up her pillow. She brought the pillow to where her mama was.

"Do you remember this?" she asked as she held the pillow extended from her right hand.

"Yes! That's my pillow," Ann said.

"It became mine when you left. You see, Mama, I sleep with it every night and take it everywhere I go," said Maud.

Maud related the story of the pillow to her mama. "It started when I was three years old. Grandma brought me over to your bed. She said I woke up crying every morning. Crying for hours, she said I probably missed you, having separation anxiety.

"The pillow didn't replace you. Instead, it filled my lungs with your scent—the scent of your bosom, the scent a child misses and craves for every night and morning," Maud said with a grin then a proud smile.

"At seven years old, I could identify the different scents on the pillow: breast milk, your sweat and your unique smell, your dirt and grime, and hundreds of hair follicles I pulled from the pillow. At this age, the pillow was like my mother. It replaced her. I would kiss the pillow when I leave for school and return. I would sniff the pillow, filling my lungs and heart every night before going to bed. It was as if you were always here with me, protecting and comforting me. In times of sadness and pain, I could always turn to the pillow and would feel supported and loved."

Ann's eyes grew watery and red from crying. She didn't know what to think. She thought, *What a great story: a child and a pillow surviving without her mother*. Ann was sad for leaving her daughter eight years too many. She planned to do whatever it takes to be the loving mother moving forward.

Jon walked over to where Ann and Maud were sitting. He stretched his hand out to them, binding their hands with his, making a ring. He listened as his daughter talked of The Kites of Love. Jon and Ann set their eyes on Maud's face as she told the story of flying kites. They watched as her facial features transformed the story along with the gestures of her hands.

"The pillow and its smell played a significant part in my life. I was strongly attached to the pillow, and love for the pillow was for my mother. I had to find her. It consumed me and led me to do whatever it takes to bring her home.

Andrew, the next-door neighbor, introduced me to kite fly-ing. I flew my first kite and saw how far it went in the atmo-sphere. The physics of the kite flying, the lift, tension, and drag, convinced me that kite flying was the way to communi-cate to get to my parents. I needed many kites and many kite flyers. My cousins and friends helped. We flew eighty-five kites at a lookout peak west of the harvest house during the eye of the hurricane. We released our energies into the kites and asked God to guide them to you, and he did."

Maud took a deep breath from talking as she gazed up, looking in her parents' faces. Their tears were running down their faces and falling off their cheek onto their necks. They couldn't wipe the tears fast enough. It was like a dripping pipe. Maud asked if she should continue as her eyes became watery too from looking into her parents' eyes.

"Yes, yes!" they cried.

"Mama and Papa, I miss you very much. My life without you was lacking with a mother's and father's love. Grandma took care of me the best way she knew how, but it's not the same. I guess I'm different, but the scent of a mother and father never leaves you. Now my life is complete. I have my mother, father, and grandma. I love you."

Maud looked up at the zinc ceiling as if it wasn't there; talking to God in heaven, with a cry of gratitude, she said, "I will lift up mine eyes unto the hill from whence cometh my help, my help cometh from the Lord."

Ann's and Jon's emotions were boiling. Their crying could be heard among the others in the house. There were tears of triumph. Fiercely proud of their daughter's accomplishment, they embraced her and said, "Thank you, thank you, daughter."

Everybody was full from eating and were celebrating. The night ended, and another chapter began.

* * *

The Kites of Love crew arrived in Saint Ann two days later. Ann was excited to see her mother. She waited on the tiny veranda so as to not frighten her mama walking in the house.

Maud walked in the house, greeted her grandma, unruffled as she spoke, trying not to give away the surprise. Maud was calm as she spoke. It wasn't easy preparing her grandmother for the news of eight years of her life—eight years of not having her daughter at home. Maud broke the news, counting every word as she spoke. "The kite flying was a success. The Kites of Love was successful. We did it, Grandma. Mama and Papa are here. They found the kites in Cuba."

"What do you mean?" Grandma said as she interrupted Maud.

"They are here, Grandma. They traveled on a ship from Cuba to Jamaica and mule carts to here," Maud said.

"Here in Saint Ann, here at the house!" Grandma shouted.

MamaJames brushed back her hair with her hands and straightened her clothes. Her steps were slow as she walked to the door. Her heart was pounding and her hands were shaking as she reached for the doorknob. The sun's powerful ray shone on the veranda, blinding MamaJames. She held her hands in the air, blocking the direct sunlight from her eyes. The image of a man and a woman stood on the veranda. MamaJames couldn't recognize the two people.

"Mama, it's me, Ann!"

Ann held her mama's hand as she pulled her back into the house, away from the sun. "Oh my...oh my god. Ann, it's you, you are here!"

"Yes, Mama, it's us, Ann and Jon!"

The two women, mother and daughter, hugged each other, locked in embrace as the tears of jubilation covered their faces. Her prayers were answered. "Thank you, God. Thank you, God, for this miracle," she said as she hugged her daughter with one hand and the other hand was in the air, acknowledging her Lord.

"Oh, I am so weak. My knees are shaking," said MamaJames.

Jon and Ann helped MamaJames to sit.

Having her daughter and son-in-law here at home was all MamaJames prayed and hoped for. She never expected her body would react this way.

"I am so tired," MamaJames said.

Her heart was beating out of her chest; she was out of breath. "I felt like I was running, running very hard."

MamaJames took a sip of water to wet her throat. She held her daughter's hands, rubbing it as she talked. "I am so happy you're home. I love you so much." Her voice was filled with tears—tears of happiness. She was smiling as her tears fell from her eyes.

Jon and Andrew helped MamaJames into the mule cart as they took the trip home to Saint Mary. Maud and her mother sandwiched Grandma in the cart as they traveled home; they sang the chorus of "Amazing Grace" all the way home until they drove into their yard.

The evening and days that followed were filled with chatter and laughter, as they all settled in and caught up on old times. MamaJames invited the whole family to go to church to celebrate the homecoming of her daughter and her son-in-law. During the church ceremony, the pastor asked the congregation to come forward for special prayers. MamaJames and the family went up to the front of the church. After the pastor prayed for everyone, they returned to their seats, except for MamaJames. She waited for the pastor. They spoke, then he prayed for her again.

MamaJames walked back to her seat. Her walk was filled with grace, her head was held high, and each step was straight and quick as she rejoined her family. It was as if all her ailment was gone and she was healed. She looked at peace with herself, at peace with God.

* * *

It was a Tuesday morning. The sun peeked through the window in MamaJames's room. She was still lying on her bed. She never slept past the sunrise. She was usually up early to make breakfast and see Maud off to school.

"Say goodbye to Grandma for me, Mama," said Maud.

Ann felt that her mother was tired and wanted to rest longer.

It was after 6:00 a.m. when Ann decided to wake her mother up. "Mama, Mama!" she called, shaking her mother. Her body was cool to the touch; there was no breath from her nose or mouth. "Mama! Mama is dead! Jon, Jon, my mama is dead!" she called out to her husband.

Jon ran inside. "What! Mama is dead?"

"Yes!" cried Ann.

Jon went to get the doctor and picked up Maud from school.

The district doctor pronounced MamaJames dead.

* * *

Maud was surprised when her papa picked her up from school. She thought that this was unusual; however, she was happy to see her papa until he told her the bad news: "Grandma died this morning."

Maud was saddened by the news of her grandma's passing. The weight of the sorrow in her heart was too much to bear for her upper body. Maud fainted and fell to the ground from the shock of the news. Jon shook his daughter vigorously until she became responsive. He then lay on the ground next to her in silence for a while.

Maud arrived home. MamaJames was dead and was lying on her bed. The coroner hadn't removed the body yet. Maud sat by her grandma's body. With tears in her eyes she said, "I miss you and love you, Grandma. Goodbye. I just got my parents back. Our family was whole again, and now I lost Grandma." Maud turned to her parents for an answer.

"That's how God works. Grandma was sick for a long time. She waited for us to return. Her illness might have been very grave, but she held on. She prayed to God to give her the strength to see us return before she died, and he did," Ann said. "I know you're sad and missing Grandma, but you have to be thankful for all the things that Grandma did for this family. We all have to travel the road of life from birth to death. Grandma did. Now we have to carry on her legacy."

Grandma was buried a month later. Families and friends from all over Jamaica attended.

CHAPTER 15

Ann sold a couple rolls of fabric at the fabric store in Morant Bay. She used a portion of the money to buy a sewing machine. The other four rolls she used to start her dressmaking business.

Jon and Ann lived in their mother's house that was passed down from MamaJames's estate. They allowed Andrew to continue leasing their property, as the money was a big help.

Jon had gained a new skill in Cuba, a talent he never knew he had: cutting hair. He bought some haircutting tools to start a barber shop. Jon would trim the plantation workers' hair. He surprised himself at this new skill and improved as he trimmed more hair; he called it a newfound talent.

Maud gave her mother back her pillow. "I have you now, Mama, the real deal."

Maud slept on her grandma's pillow. With every sniff, she inhaled the memories of her grandmother.

Maud proposed to Andrew to help her make a kite in memory of The Kites of Love. The kite was bigger than any of the kites they had made. They wrote the names of everyone that took part in The Kites of Love and added their parents' and cousin Samuel's names to the kite, completing its purpose.

* * *

It was a bedtime story night at the Brown's house as Andrew and Maud sat around the wood fire, telling their nine children the story of a very important chapter in their lives.

The Brown family gazed up on the wall. There was an enormous kite frame in a lignum vitae wood hanging from the wall: The Kites of Love.

The End

ABOUT THE AUTHOR

Enadene McFarlane was born in Kingston, Jamaica, and started writing poems at a young age.

She continued writing poems and short stories after she moved to the United States. She lived in South Florida with her son.

After many years in South Florida, she moved to Waterloo, Iowa, working in the human service field. There, she met her husband. They lived in rural Waterloo surrounded by a cornfield. When it wasn't snowing, the beautiful planes of the countryside were visible as far as the eyes could see. Iowa gave her the drive and the mindset to start the novel *The Kites of Love*.

She moved back to Florida, the diversity of the sunshine state, and put a spin on her style of writing. She completed *The Kites of Love*.

Her happiness is in Florida with her family.

Printed in the USA
CPSIA information can be obtained
at www.ICGtesting.com
LVHW020345100624
782716LV00012B/403